IN THIS
LIVING
BODY

M. J. SULLIVAN

想究竟涅槃三世諸佛依般若波羅蜜多故

得阿耨多羅三藐三菩提故知般若波羅蜜

多是大神呪是大明呪是無上呪是無等等

呪能除一切苦真實不虛故説般若波羅蜜

多呪即説呪曰

羯諦羯諦 波羅羯諦 波羅僧羯諦

菩提娑婆呵

般若心經

辛卯年 弥生

聖峯 謹書

摩訶般若波羅蜜多心経

観自在菩薩行深般若波羅蜜多時照見五

蘊皆空度一切苦厄舎利子色不異空空不

異色色即是空空即是色受想行識亦復如

是舎利子是諸法空相不生不滅不垢不浄

不増不減是故空中無色無受想行識無眼

耳鼻舌身意無色聲香味觸法無眼界乃至

無意識界無無明亦無無明盡乃至無老死

亦無老死盡無苦集滅道無智亦無得以無

所得故菩提薩埵依般若波羅蜜多故心無

罣礙無罣礙故無有恐怖遠離一切顛倒夢

Shingyō, The Heart Sutra
Seihō, 2011

ALSO BY M. J. SULLIVAN

Seihō's Kanji Workbook

Sword and Psyche

WAZA

Japanese Calligraphy: Practice, Learning, and Art
(with the calligraphy of Harada Kampō)

Japanese Calligraphy: A First Year Curriculum
(with the calligraphy of Harada Kampō)

Velvet (with Alec Kalla)

Silk and Steel

Shingyō: Reflections on Translating the Heart Sutra

IN THIS LIVING BODY

M. J. Sullivan

SILVERBACK SAGES

This is a true story. Most of the facts and names have been changed in order to allow it to be true. Most of the places and all of the dreams are described as accurately as possible. *However*:

This is a work of fiction. All of the characters, organizations, and events portrayed in the book are either products of the author's imagination or are used fictionally.

ISBN 978-0-9829920-1-2
LCCN: 2012945559

1. Japan-Fiction. 2. Zen practice-Fiction. 3. Martial arts-Fiction. 4. Foreigner in Japan-Fiction. 5. Sensei student-Fiction. 6. Guru disciple-Fiction. 7. Buddhism (philosophy)-Fiction. 8. Mummification-Fiction. 9. Japanese religions-Fiction. 10. Elasticity of time (psychology)-Fiction. 11. Prophetic dreams (psychology)-Fiction. 12. Takamatsu (city in Japan)-Fiction. 13. Mountains of Shikoku-Fiction. 14. Rihaku (Li Po)-Fiction. 15. Kukai (Kobo Daishi)-Fiction. 16. The Heart Sutra (Shingyo)-Fiction. 17. Suppression of Buddhism under Meiji-Fiction.

I Title.

Cover design, Copyright © 2014, Silverback Sages Publishers.
Illustrations, Copyright © 2011, Tōshoin Studio.
Author photo courtesy Colorado Academy of Martial Arts

Printed in The United States of America

IN THIS LIVING BODY

"... if we go to the mystic himself and ask for information about what he has experienced, he will tell us that he cannot tell us, and then he will tell us."

Holmes Welch,
Taoism: The Parting of the Way

い

The old priest's eyes are glittering onyx gems that look not at him but into him. Under that gaze his suitcase is no longer heavy and he's no longer worn with long travel. He is suddenly alert and present and not tired at all.

Terayama I am, the old man says, bowing. Pleased to meet you for the first time.

West I am, he answers, bowing too, the first words he has spoken since boarding the ferry in Kobê. He speaks in Japanese, his English name sounding awkwardly inserted. Pleased to meet you for the first time.

He sees the priest whole now, not just the eyes, wearing dark robes, wizened, hairless, yet standing un-bent, the statue of an ancient warrior.

He steps out into the damp night, still breathing salt air from the harbor, sees the parking circle and the street and the ruined medieval castle beyond through the mist lit by cloudy halogen. It is humid and the smells of wet grass and pavement mix with the sea air. A few taxis wait, rain-spattered and with their soft yellow roof signs glowing.

Quickly if you please, the old man says, pointing to the taxis.

They get into one of them, just out of the detail shop and complete with scent. Terayama asks the driver to go to the Hachiman Shrine. To pay our respects, he says to West.

The taxi leaves them under a tall concrete arch before a gracefully curved concrete bridge spanning a stagnant moat. It is just then six in the morning and the first of the sun fades the streetlights. A great bell tolls six times somewhere to the south of them. They cross the bridge on foot and pass under an intricately carved wooden gate. The gate is flanked by guardhouses manned by painted statues of seated archers wearing fierce iron masks and antique armor. On the damp ground a mossy stone walkway leads them up to the outer shrine building. A shaft of early sunlight enters the park behind them, brightens the plethora of greens and fits them into the pattern of long deep tree shadows smelling of the recent rain. Before them at the end of the path a tall wood and thatch shrine looms. He follows Terayama up the steps. The eaves and columns are carved with clouds and dragons, mythical beasts and demons, from a time before self-conscious time. A number of bobtailed cats lounge or play under the porch and stairs.

Terayama bows and claps his hands twice. West does the same. Then Terayama pulls a thick cord dangling from the eaves, bringing the tinkle of a bell from somewhere deep inside the building. He throws a coin into a grate-covered box. Then they bow and clap again.

Hachiman-san is the God of War, Terayama whispers.

Their walk back to Hachiman Street covers centuries, from the barely historic to the now. Once onto the pavement they pass two coffeehouses with modern façades that are open. Terayama shows no interest in them. On a side street they come to a small place behind a latticed wooden sliding door. Workmen in their baggy trousers over split-toed socks and one man in kimono are in there sitting at low tables and eating from bowls. They find an empty table and sit. A tiny old woman in a brown kimono and white apron and a cloth wrapped around her head welcomes them and asks what they want. Terayama orders a set breakfast for West, a cup of hot water for himself. As they wait West basks in the atmosphere of the place, the dim light through paper windows, everyone there but himself in costume from earlier times. The set breakfast arrives on a tray bearing a brown soup, a bowl of rice, some boiled vegetables, a few pickles, a small whole fish, a cup of tea.

They fold their hands. Terayama mutters a brief chant, pulls a small bag from his left sleeve. It holds an assortment of nuts, some dried brown nettles. He nibbles on these, sips his cup of hot water. They eat in silence. When they have finished they again fold their hands and Terayama mutters another short phrase. West repeats it, having used it before. Terayama closes his bag of nuts and returns it to his sleeve, speaks at last.

Tired, are you? he asks.

A little, Sensei, West admits.

Then I will show you to your apartment and you can rest.

Will we need a taxi? West asks.

No. It is right next to the Hachiman Shrine.

They walk back to the entrance of the shrine. West watches the city of Takamatsu awakening, modern and old, side by side. Colorful umbrellas are everywhere. Women in traditional dress walk or carry in swaddling backpacks tiny, darling children. One little boy of four or five stomps gaily in a large puddle. His mother laughs. Men in business suits ride by on rusty bicycles. Two old men wearing dark kimono and French beret shuffle along in close conversation. A Buddhist priest in robes similar to Terayama's wends his way through traffic on a Honda motorscooter.

The apartment building is of pre-stressed concrete, from the immediate post-war era. They climb the three exposed flights of iron stairs. At one of the two steel doors on that floor Terayama produces a key. They enter and remove their shoes.

The small vestibule is surrounded by doors. Terayama opens each of them to give him a peek, one to the bath, one to the toilet, one to the kitchen and one to the front room. That door is the traditional sliding type made of heavy paper on a light wood frame. In it West sees tatami, four and a half mats, a bit over nine by nine feet. The tatami smells of freshly mown hay. A small low table has been placed below the shoji paper window. Apart from the kitchen and bath, the modern era is absent here. West has stepped back into Meiji or even earlier. He slides stocking feet across the tatami, opens the shoji screen, sees the moat directly below him, the tree-shaded grounds of the shrine to his left, all gilded by shafts of early morning sunlight.

How beautiful it is, he blurts. He is surprised to hear that he has spoken in Japanese. Terayama does not comment, but joins him at the window. They look together at the scene below. A frog jumps into the moat. A mallard drake quacks at it. The old priest and the tall foreigner share a joyful glance and bright smiles.

Terayama shows him the rolled bedding in the closet behind paper sliding doors. With clean quick movements he lays out the futon and the pillows and the quilt. Then he sits on his heels and signs West to do the same, facing him.

Yamazaki-san will want to see you in the office tomorrow, he says. There are always cabs. You have the address. Once you have been there you will get a bicycle and be able to use it instead. Rest now.

They bow. West thanks him. Terayama withdraws without turning his back, draws shut the door to the vestibule. West remains sitting until he hears the outer steel door close. He returns to his window and watches for the old man, but it seems he has gone a way West cannot follow, at least not with his eyes.

ろ

A single cab sits in the early sun under the shrine's great arch. As he approaches it the rear door opens. He thinks it is the same driver from the day before but isn't sure.

As for yesterday's morning, taxi you drove?

Where to? the driver asks.

Yesterday's morning?

Now.

West shrugs, says Marugame-machi. The driver starts the meter, turns north.

West is preoccupied, thinking about how he will present himself at Yamazaki Industries. He is not in the present, pays no real attention to the streets, the thin traffic, the occasional pedestrian. They cross a bridge over the rail lines into a neighborhood of weathered wooden shops and houses. No cars, trucks. A few women in kimono sweep and mop cobbled stoops. A man in a short jacket and leggings tied into straw sandals pushes a cart with wood wheels. No one looks at the cab.

Near the end of the street a man emerges from the shadows of a paneled entrance. His forehead is shaved, his long hair in an oiled bun. He is sliding his second sheathed sword into his wide sash. The shoulders of his kimono spread into points left and right, the wings of a falcon.

As for here, Marugame-machi is it? he asks.

His voice is thick, he is chilled, frightened. This is a 17th century street, a Ukiyoe print, The wrong time. He scans for cameras, kliegs, reflectors, proof that this is a movie set. Sees nothing.

The driver doesn't speak, just turns the cab into the traffic on a busy modern street heading east, then south over the tracks again. In a few minutes he stops under a covered intersection. A few people walk or cycle on the cross-street under the translucent roofing that extends overhead both north and south.

Marugame-machi, the driver says, opening the automatic door. He seems to try to keep his face averted as West pays him, but not successfully. West is certain he'll know him if he sees him again.

He is still shaken by the detour into an earlier time. He pays close attention now, to an old woman in kimono pushing a chromed shopping cart, two housewives in western clothes nattering as they window shop, a young man in a business suit pedaling his bicycle furiously, clearly late for work. He sees the Yamazaki Industries logo half a block ahead, red on white, almost glowing.

On the ground floor is a retail computer shop, its glass front plastered with lightning-shaped Japanese versions of italics in screaming colors. Inside it is quiet, subdued, thick-carpeted and meticulously clean and orderly. Rows of computers and components on pedestals, software disks presented in satin-lined cases. Calming as it is all meant to be, this jump into the twenty-first century disturbs him greatly.

He is greeted softly by a young woman wearing a dark navy miniskirt and black spike heels, a powder blue smock over a crisp white blouse. She bows in welcome, asks in a whisper what she can do for him. He bows too, tells her he wishes to see Yamazaki Hiroshi, the bucho. Bucho, is that correct?

Her very red mouth forms an O, her eyes widen. Ah, she says, West-san you are perhaps?

He admits that he is. She bows again and assures him that bucho is correct, means branch chief, then leads him back outside into the late Showa era of Marugame-machi's covered pedestrian street and to an unmarked door, next to the left. This opens into a cramped, unfurnished lobby from a '50s L.A. film noir, where a narrow hallway sneaks past a steep staircase. Go up please, she says. He thanks her and bows and she bows and he hears her heels and the sigh of the door once he is halfway up the stairs.

At the top is a hall with a linoleum floor and blank walls punctuated with a row of doors all marked Yamazaki Industries, black characters painted on mottled glass. He tries several and finds them locked. The last one, nearest the back of the building, opens onto a room from the Taisho era, 19th century Dickens, scarred plank floor, two rows of three battered face-to-face wooden desks with pigeon holes, all dust-free and recently polished. No one is there. A door at the far end of the room stands open. Yamazaki-bucho? West asks.

A man stands from behind a desk in the room beyond, backlit by a dirty casement window. West-san are you? Come in.

They bow, recite their formal exchanges.

You studied karate with my brother in San Francisco, says Hiroshi Yamazaki in perfect English. He has recommended you highly.

I'm very grateful to Yamazaki Takeshi-sensei, West says. Coming here fulfills a dream. To study karate in Japan.

Yes. Well, to stay for a long time you have to have a job to keep your visa. So you will work here.

I am very grateful to you for that, too.

They are silent for an edgy time. The office is cramped, stuffy, littered with computer print-outs and broken pieces of computer hardware. Yamazaki appears rumpled, tired. His hair is long, shaggy, not very clean. His eyes are hooded, seem to land everywhere but on West's. Not knowing where to look himself,

West turns to the dirty second-floor window, examines the translucent covering over the busy narrow street. Motes dance in a slanted shaft of hazy morning sunlight.

Finally Yamazaki says, Terayama-sensei is not famous at all. The Senkyo Sect is very private. Very secret.

Why? West asks.

I don't know. Something to do with religion.

Another long pause. Below the window West thinks he sees Terayama ride by on a bicycle, but he isn't sure.

You will find your bicycle in the lobby under the staircase, Yamazaki says. It is the black one. Can you find your way home alone?

Yes, I'm sure I can.

You can park the bicycle in the shed behind the apartment building. There are shops near your apartment. A Marunaka supermarket.

Yes.

All right then, Yamazaki says. Come back tomorrow and we'll find something for you to do.

He finds his bicycle, wheels it out into the Marugame-machi. His way takes him through the Hyogo-machi's covered shopping streets, lined with a fascinating variety of stores selling kimono, Buddhist religious objects, a modern drugstore, a hardware store displaying traditional tools with wonderfully carved wooden handles, a shop stacked to the ceiling with electrical kitchen appliances which pours loud pop music into the street, a Pachinko parlor complete with a pair of gangsters dressed like George Raft in the 40s loitering outside. Once he is out from under the cover he is jarred by the rush of heavy traffic clogging the main north-south street.

He is about to ride south there on the broad sidewalk when he definitely sees Terayama on a bicycle. He is dressed in a blue track suit with white stripes down the sleeves and legs, wears running shoes and a blue ball cap. He looks like a youthful athlete with a dark complexion and deep wrinkles. He signals West to turn right and follow him onto a narrow brick street.

Terayama slows and points as they pass a martial arts supply shop. West nods that he has noted it. They turn north for a few blocks and then back to the west on a major thoroughfare. Terayama again slows and points out a shop specializing in traditional painting and calligraphy materials. Again West nods. A few blocks later they turn north once more. A short distance up that street Terayama stops, dismounts and lifts his bike onto a stand next to a wooden gate in an old stone wall. West does the same. Across the street is the Prefectural Office building, a gray arrangement of planes and angles, a famous example of twentieth-century architecture.

He follows the old man as he slips through a small gate beside the large one, onto the grounds of a sort of park. Standing tall in there is a bronze Amida Buddha. Beyond that is a walkway leading to a small meditation hall in the Zen style. They are now as far back as the Muromachi Period, surrounded by the organic shapes and subtle colors of the fourteenth century. West feels strange that they are wearing modern western clothes.

At the front of the hall Terayama bows, opens the sliding wooden door, waves West in. They remove their shoes on the flagstone floor of the vestibule. Terayama slides open the plain dun paper door and they step up onto old wood and enter the hall. A meter wide length of wooden floor runs down the center between two rows of tatami mats lined up on platforms a foot higher, eight on either side. At the end is another mat, framed by rectangular wood pillars. On it are arranged an incense burner, a wooden fish-shaped gong, some small wooden blocks. The wall behind it is blank.

The sound of the city's traffic seems to emphasize the quiet of the place. He remembers that it had been the same at the

Zen center in California, the feeling that the hectic activity of the fleeting world is of no consequence. Here, that feeling envelops him ten-fold.

They bow and sit on the tatami and breathe for several minutes. Finally Terayama bows from his seat, rises, bows again and leaves. West follows. Back in the stone-floored vestibule Terayama points to a sign brushed in clear calligraphy which says that meditation training takes place there at five in the morning every Tuesday and Thursday. West nods. They return to their bicycles and ride south.

They regain territory familiar to West. Terayama points out the Marunaka supermarket and West nods. Then a little restaurant specializing in domburi. West nods. A dry cleaner's. West nods. Another turn or two and they are in front of the Hachiman Shrine. Terayama waves goodbye and disappears around a corner pedaling furiously.

West can't help chuckling. Not one word. The best tour guide he's ever known.

He wends his bike around to the rack under the shed behind his apartment building, racks it there and goes up, unlocks the steel door, enters, removes his shoes. He goes for the first time into his back room and is surprised. It is a six-mat room, about nine by twelve feet. Along the east wall a rudimentary wood and bamboo alcove, a kind of private shrine with nothing in it, waiting for a Buddha or a scroll. The great bell rings its twelve noon strokes. He opens the shoji screen that faces south. Sliding glass doors behind the screen open onto a tiny balcony and overlook the elevated tracks of the JNR there, the rails flashing in the sun. A Buddhist cemetery on the slope rises toward dense forest far beyond. He slides open the door, sees the bell high among the stones. Moments after its last tolling a train whistle blows and then the train passes eastbound, roaring and clattering over the trestle. He smiles. Do they time the trains for a few minutes before or after the bells?

A glass-fronted bookcase stands in a corner, full of books in Japanese. He rummages among them, finds a Takamatsu guidebook with a map of the city. He finds the shrine, his own apartment building, Marugame-machi. There was no reason for the cab to cross the tracks to get him from one to the other.

A low table surrounded by cushions has two books on it with a handwritten note peeking out from under them. The first book is a primer on Senkyo style karate. The second is a privately printed treatise on swordsmanship. The note reads, *Memorize the characters.*

The kitchen proves to be well equipped but not well stocked. In a cabinet he finds a can of tuna and a can of mackerel and three packets of dehydrated ramen and one of dried seaweed, a small bag of green tea. He finds nothing in the fridge. He makes a lunch out of some of it, sits to eat at the low table in the six mat room, glances over the karate text. He knows the terms but has never seen them written in Japanese. He looks for pen and paper, finds some in a drawer at the bottom of the bookcase. In the bookcase itself he finds the Nelson Japanese Character Dictionary. He finishes with his bowl and chopsticks and washes them out in the sink and returns to the table and goes to work.

He hears the bell ring six times and then the whistle and the noise of the westbound train. He has arranged his notes on the karate characters, lays them aside, looks into the book on swordsmanship. This is entirely new to him and his eyes are tired. He rises stiffly and stretches cramped legs and sketches a few karate exercises.

He goes to his window above the moat and watches life below at the entrance to the shrine. He leans out and to the left and through the trees can just see the main hall, where all sorts of people bow, clap twice to rouse the god, and pray. Young men in karate uniforms, preparing for a test or tournament. Old women in kimono, mourning a lost relative. Kids in their semi-military school uniforms, worried about an entrance exam. Men in dark pinstripes, concerned about a promotion, a business deal. He listens to the ducks in the moat, distant traffic, the occasional greetings between married women carrying infants in bundles on their backs as they walk to or from shopping in the street below. This is joy, he thinks. This is home.

は

He cycles through a gray morning mist to Yamazaki Industries at what he hopes will be the right time. Racks his bicycle, takes the stairs. He looks around the gloomy worn-out room. A dowdy young woman is dusting. She hears the door, turns in alarm, recovers and bows. A bald man with hornrims looks up from his desk and nods. An athletic looking fellow at another desk does not look up. The door to Yamazaki's office is closed.

West I am, he says. Yamazaki-bucho, is he here?

There is a brief silence. The woman says that he is here, but he is busy. Would West-san care for tea?

He says he would, and thank you. She points out an empty desk, signals him to sit. There are no papers on the desk. It has a row of small filing slots, all empty. The bald man's desk faces his. He looks over the filing slots, nods again.

Ikeda, I am, he says.

West, I am. Pleased to meet you for the first time.

The woman brings his tea. Oka, I am, she says.

Pleased to meet you for the first time.

He sips tea and waits. He has finished all but the cold dregs of his tea when he hears the scrape of a chair behind him. He hears steps, senses someone standing beside him. He turns and looks up. It is the athletic fellow, about his own age or a little younger.

Hirano, I am, the younger man says. Pleased to meet you for the first time, West-san.

Pleased to meet you for the first time, Hirano-san.

Perhaps you would like to read a magazine, would you?

Yes, thank you.

Hirano hands him a martial arts magazine in Japanese. Read this, can you? he asks.

A little of it. Enough for now, I think. Thank you.

Hirano withdraws and West turns back to his desk and the magazine. It is about swordsmanship. He finds an article that is about the same school of swordsmanship that the treatise on his table at home discussed. One of the pictures is of Terayama, in the classic split skirts and jacket and wielding a long Samurai sword. He reads what he can. The article does not refer to Terayama as Terayama, but as Reikyo. At least he thinks that is how the characters are pronounced. Their meaning is Spirit Doctrine.

Finally there are sounds from behind Yamazaki's door. The man steps out into the room, more rumpled and bleary than even he'd been the day before.

West-san, he says. Met everyone, have you?

Yes sir.

Good.

Then to Ikeda he says, Give him something to translate into English.

Ikeda gives him a glossy pamphlet with pictures of electronic circuits. It shrieks with stylized script and many exclamation points.

I'm sorry, but I will need my dictionaries, West says.

That's all right, Yamazaki says. Take it home. Bring it back when you are finished. Ikeda-san, give him some of your English copy to edit.

Ikeda hands him a few sheets of typing.

All right, West says, I can do this now.

No hurry, Yamazaki tells him. When it's convenient. Then he announces to the office that he is going out for the afternoon. All stand and bow and say Sayonara. Once he has left, the others return to whatever is on their desks. He spends some time with Mr. Ikeda's manuscript. It is typed with an old manual typewriter and extols Yamazaki computer circuits in stilted English. He compares it with the garish brochure he has been given and decides that this is the source of the typed translation.

Excuse me, Ikeda-san, but may I ask you?

Ikeda looks over the filing slots. Yes, he says.

Excuse me, but this is the translation of the brochure, is it?

Yes, it is.

Thank you.

He returns to reading the manuscript. It is accurately translated he is sure, but stiff and without punch. He is not sure what he should do. If the translation were to work as American advertising copy, it would need complete revision. But he doesn't want to offend Mr. Ikeda. So he spends more time with the brochure, identifying passages as Ikeda has translated them, copying the characters on a separate sheet with their meanings in English. Miss Oka has gone to a desk with three different typewriters and is pecking away on one of them. He simply is not sure what else he can do.

Excuse me, Ikeda-san, he says again.

Yes.

For this I really will need my dictionaries.

Yes, I understand. Please take them home.

Yes, thank you, that would be best, I think.

Yes.

Tomorrow I will bring them back, he says.

Come after eleven please. As I have correspondence in the morning.

So he folds the brochure and the manuscript into his jacket pocket and puts away his pen and stands and says Arigato and Sayonara to all three, bowing, and leaves Yamazaki Industries with a sigh of relief.

に

The pre-dawn is cool and smells of trees and plants rather than of trains or traffic. The tires of his bicycle hiss on the pavement and there is a sharp squawk from one of the pedals. He finds his way through the darkened streets to the Zen temple, gets there five minutes before five. He racks his bike next to several others. The gate is open. He walks quickly past the tall bronze Buddha, who gazes across to the modern Prefectural office building with perfect equanimity. When he reaches the hall he sees a businessman in the flagstone vestibule removing his shoes. The sliding door to the hall is open. One or two office ladies, a college student, and Hirano in a black tracksuit are sitting on pillows in one or another degree of the Lotus position or sitting on their heels. He is surprised to see Hirano there, though he realizes there is no good reason for that. No one looks up when he enters and takes a place on the tatami mat nearest the door, arranges the pillows he finds there and sits. One other person enters and arranges himself across the aisle, the last one. Then silence.

He sees that preparations have been made on the dais. A scroll has been hung. An arrangement of fresh flowers flanks the wooden gong and a pillow has been placed dead center of all of it. It is a pleasing picture. The scroll is large and bordered with two contrasting silk brocades framing a single character brushed boldly and wildly to fill its entire paper center. It reads *Emptiness.*

The priest enters. West realizes that he has half expected Terayama-sensei, but this is not he. This priest's head is shaved as is Terayama's, and he wears a similar brown robe with the strap over the shoulder, but he is much younger, perhaps forty. He moves smoothly to his cushion, seats himself and arranges his robes gracefully. He looks out over the rest of the hall, spots West. Nudges the woman seated nearest him, whispers. She rises, reaches behind her for something, walks silently to West and hands him a small white pamphlet. He bows from his seat, raising the pamphlet to his forehead. She bows, returns to her seat.

The priest puts a match to the incense and soon sandalwood gently fills the air. West closes his eyes and from within him, not from within him he knows but from the belly of the priest, comes a sound that jolts his body, a huge, deep, penetrating sound, he sits stunned, he has heard recordings but this is entirely other than they ever were, gradually he can distinguish syllables, *Ma ka han nya ha ra mi ta shin gyō.* The *gyō* strings out in time, drops in pitch until it is a growl that disappears into West's body and sticks there. Then he hears the sound of the wooden gong and the voices of all around him and realizes that this is what the pamphlet is for, he is to chant with them. He finally finds his place, or thinks he does, but he loses the rhythm, he will have to practice, so he just listens and lets the sounds carry him, wherever they are going he will go.

At a point all the voices stop but that of the priest and that alone intones the last four syllables, *Han ya shin gyō,* the *gyō* again extended and dropping in pitch to a growl.

Silence follows. He knows what to do with that, he has learned to follow the breath, empty the mind. He meditates. They all meditate. On *Emptiness.*

He has gone entirely empty and beyond time when he is

shocked out of himself by a loud crack of wood on wood. He starts, looks toward the source of the sound. The priest is putting away the pair of wooden blocks he'd noticed there on the dais when he'd entered. The people around him stir, change posture, rub dead feet or knees. He does the same. In a few minutes they gradually resume their formal postures. He does the same. The priest lights a fresh stick of incense and strikes the wooden gong and they chant again and again he tries to find his place in the pamphlet and fails and so just listens. A different chant this time, this one almost intelligible as Japanese, but not modern Japanese, forget the words forget the grammar hear just the sound the heart of the sound the hearts in the sound.

When this chant ends they sit again in silence, meditate again. It is the same this time, he soon disappears inside, it is so peaceful, so quiet. Then the crack of the wooden blocks, this time perhaps not quite so shocking, no one shifts this time, but all immediately follow the priest who chants *Shi gu sei gan mon,* as it happens he knows this one from the Zen center in the States, the only one they chanted in Japanese rather than English. It is very short and so he can join in. When it is over, everyone uncoils and rubs feet and knees, and one man opens the shoji blinds to the south and they see the start of dawn backlighting the city hall and some other buildings. No one speaks. They file out slowly in ones and twos, retrieve their shoes from the cabinet in the vestibule, walk out into the new day. West is last. He finds Hirano waiting for him.

Good morning, Hirano says.

Good morning, Hirano-san.

Next time wear rough clothes. You have hours before work.

Yes. I didn't know.

You are skilled in sitting.

For me it is not difficult. I attended meditation at a Zen

center in California for some years.

Do you want to study karate while you are here?

Yes. It's the main reason I came. But it must be the school of karate Terayama-sensei follows.

Senkyo style. Yes, that is ours. Good. The classes are on Monday, Wednesday and Friday. Tomorrow evening after work, I will take you if you want.

Yes, thank you very much.

You will just watch this first time. Then the teacher will talk with you and decide if he will accept you as a student.

I understand. Excuse me, but, Hirano-san, can you tell me about a street north of the railroad? Perhaps Tokugawa Period, it appears, with people dressed as from that time?

Hirano looks at him with narrowed eyes, then smiles a little. Rekishi-machi, he says. History Street. You went there?

No. The taxi took me there on the way to Yamazaki Industries. It was not really on the way.

Yes, it is not. I have seen it.

He pauses, ponders. Then says, It is not always of the Tokugawa time. When I saw it, it was from the time of Meiji. One young student said he saw it during Showa, on fire from the American bombing.

West drops his gaze. Several seconds pass before he can speak.

Is it for the movies? he asks at last.

Hirano looks away, His eyes first on the tall buddha, then at the rooftop of the Prefectural office building. West waits, wondering what the man is seeing.

No, he says. Well, see you at the office, then.

Until later.

He watches Hirano's walk. Yes, he can see that he is a karate man, the straight posture, the smooth and easy movement. Excellent.

Then he blinks and looks through the trees at the tall Buddha and smiles to himself. What a beautiful morning. What a wonderful day.

ほ

It is far too early for him to go to the office, so he goes to the apartment and changes into his other suit, has a breakfast of tea and leftover rice with some seaweed and vinegar in it. He reads over the corrections he has made in Mr. Ikeda's translation, worries that the man will be offended. His English has been accurate and grammatical but is very dull indeed. West wonders how he will present his changes politely.

He cycles to work then, pausing to leave his wrinkled suit at the cleaners on the way. When he gets there he goes to his desk, says a soft Good Morning to Mr. Ikeda, who today seems to have a twinkle in his eye visible over his horn rims. He smiles a little as West sits down. No one else is in the office. He settles.

Excuse me, Ikeda-san, he says. Might I speak with you about your translation?

Ikeda gives him a tentative yes. West takes the papers and walks around to Ikeda's desk. May I speak in English? he asks.

Yes. Please.

So he first tells him that his translation was very good, very accurate in every respect. Then he tries to explain about the style of writing, the difference between simply clear, accurate English and advertising copy. Ikeda nods and nods, makes no comment. Finally he says thank you, I understand. Then West asks if this is the sort of work he will be expected to do for

Yamazaki Industries.

I don't know, Mr. West. Perhaps some of it.

So, what do you think I should do now?

It takes him a while to speak. He seems to be a bit embarrassed.

Perhaps, he says, coughing politely, perhaps you wouldn't mind helping me with this article in *Time* Magazine.

He hands West last week's *Time*, opened to an article quoting an undercover cop who describes his capture of a most-wanted criminal. He is describing his fears as he approaches the hideout on a dark night. At one point the cop says that a dog barked at a critical moment, freezing him.

Can you tell me please, Mr. Ikeda says, What does it mean, The dog's woof was a warp?

West has to think hard. What does this mean? No, I know what it means. How do I explain it?

Okay, he says when he has an idea how to do it. Woof means Bark, the sound a dog makes. Right?

Yes, I know that word.

But it also means the threads going one way in weaving cloth. And Warp means the threads going the other way, across the Woof. Do you follow that idea?

Yes. I didn't know that, Woof and Warp in weaving.

Good. Now, warp also means Bent, Curved, like a badly cured piece of wood.

Ah so. Yes, I know that one too.

Well, another way we sometimes use that meaning for Warp is in regard to Time. We speak sometimes of a Time-Warp. It means a feeling that time has gone too fast or too slow or has stopped. So the policeman heard the dog's bark, or woof, and that scared him into the feeling that time had warped. Then he used the meanings of Woof and Warp from weaving to poetically describe his feelings.

Ikeda stares in silence at his article. After half a minute or so he says shyly, Mr. West, you have just split an infinitive.

So I have, he says, amused and aback at once. Sorry.

Ikeda takes back the magazine. I see, he says. He is reading again as he speaks. Thank you. That will be most useful. I belong to a group, a kind of club. We read *Time* each week, and discuss it. To help with our English.

Yamazaki comes in, rumpled and bleary as usual, followed by Hirano. Hirano goes to his desk. He is carrying a sports bag and a briefcase. Yamazaki carries nothing, appears preoccupied, seems to lumber, has to fumble with the latch on his office door. Please send in tea, he mumbles to no one in particular. Miss Oka, whose job this would normally be, is not present, so Hirano, still on his feet, goes to the corner table where the kettle steams, brews a small pot, puts it and a cup on a tray and takes it into the office. Returns and closes the door.

In a little while Yamazaki opens the door again and sharply calls Ikeda in to see him.

Ikeda puts his magazine away and shoots West a small grin. Woof, he whispers.

As far as Mr. Ikeda is concerned, West guesses he's done what was expected of him that day for Yamazaki Industries.

The mood of the karate class is entirely different from any he's seen before. The shouts of kiai, yes, the patterns of the kata, yes, much the same. But the focus is so intense in its complete eradication of individual ego that it seems that only one elevated presence attends, not the dozen or so students. When they pair off to spar the difference is most clear. There is no dancing around, no flurry of fists or feet. There are long silences with no motion at all, just pairs of men in their white uniforms watching each other, studying each other. Then from one pair or another a sudden pounce and shout. That's all. Periodically the instructor rotates the pairs. During this phase West follows Hirano's progress. He seems to win some, to lose some. Neither he nor any of the others show any emotion toward the outcomes of these matches. They bow silently to one another, then to their next opponent. Apart from the faint sounds of shuffling on the old pine floor as they move from one match to the next there is no sound. Until the sudden kiai when someone strikes. It is eerie. The huge energy in the room is palpable, but comes not from movement or any form of speech. There is no question. This is karate as he has long hoped it would be.

At the end of the class West, at the back of the hall, kneels with the others to sit in closing meditation. He finds it immensely peaceful. Then the class ends formally and breaks up quietly, no chatting, no horseplay. Hirano invites him forward to meet the teacher.

The man is perhaps in his fifties, hard and straight and completely serious. There is no sign of sympathy or kindness in his regard of West. He looks into him as well as at him. His name is Arakawa.

You have studied this karate in America? he asks.

Not exactly like this, West says. I recognize the kata and other exercises.

What is your rank?

Shodan, in America. Here I think I should begin with no rank.

You must understand that this is not about fighting. It is about character.

Yes, Sensei. I understand.

Bring your uniform next time. I'll decide about rank after the next class.

Yes, Sensei. Thank you.

Both Arakawa-sensei and Hirano withdraw to change. The others now appear in business suits, school uniforms, sports clothes. Their demeanor is that of departing church goers, silent, introspective.

When Hirano appears he signals West to follow him. They go out to the covered street, now lit from above with strings of fluorescent tubes and the neon of the shop signs.

Shall we eat something? Hirano asks. I know a cheap restaurant that is good. Grilled fish and chicken. Other things.

Yes. That sounds good.

The restaurant is not in the Marugame-machi but in another street that has no lighting beyond a few paper lanterns in front of dim shops, a step back to the Edo period. The place is not busy. West wonders if it is late or early for dinner. They sit at a counter. Behind it is another, glass covered and iced, with a variety of fish, shellfish, and various cuts of chicken displayed.

Would you like sakê or beer? Hirano asks.

Please order for me, West says. You would know best.

Hirano orders for them both. They drink sakê as the food is being prepared. They say Kampai. Then Hirano says, So now you are in the karate class.

Yes. Thank you very much for taking me there. It's the best karate I've ever seen.

Different from in America?

Yes. Very different. But our sensei taught only the lower ranks. When the students got black belts they were sent to other schools.

It is somewhat the same here. The lower ranking students are taught on different days, and more conventional karate.

They are served, a selection of small dishes of fish and chicken. It is delicious. They pour sakê for one another as they eat. West is comfortable with his chopsticks, glad he understands the basics of Japanese table manners. Finished, they split the bill, step out into the night, walk back toward the office where they have left their bicycles. There are few shoppers left this late, and many of the stores are being shut down. A palmist has set up his table and candle in front of one of the closed shops, a young man in a suit and white shirt, no tie, eyes lowered to contemplate the text before him.

Hirano-san, I wonder if you could answer a question for me. What is it I am to do at Yamazaki Industries?

Hirano does not answer at once, seems uncertain what to answer, whether to answer. He examines a display of kimono in a shop window, coughs quietly, clears his throat.

You will not have much serious work, he says. You will translate some Japanese into English, will correct the translations Ikeda-san and I write. Usually you will just be on hand to help us to read certain passages in English, as you did today for Ikeda-san.

I see, West says, his heart sinking. All those hours to be wasted.

Hirano goes on. I would suggest that you bring your dictionaries and grammar books to work. Study. Memorize characters. It will fill the time.

I see.

Come in late. Yamazaki-bucho seldom arrives before eleven. And don't come in on Saturday. You don't have to work on Saturday.

I see. Thank you, Hirano-san.

Later, then.

Yes. Sayonara.

と

On Saturday he wakes to the six strokes of the morning bell. He has slept well on his futon. He has left open the paper doors between his two tatami rooms, giving him the feeling of great space. Soft light filters through the shoji screens. A gentle awakening.

Still in his sleeping robe, he packs the bedding into the closet, opens the shoji on his window overlooking the shrine's moat. An old woman, bent nearly in half and wearing gray kimono to match her thinning hair, shuffles across the bridge on her way to wake Hachiman-san with two claps of her hands and the ringing of the little bell and a prayer. A dozen teen age boys jog past her in formation wearing karate uniforms. They shout a kiai in unison every fourth step.

He notes that the JNR fails to snort and whistle and clatter across the trestle this morning. Seems it doesn't run on Saturday. He stretches, crosses to the shoji over the sliding doors on the south side, opens them. Mist still hangs on the high slope above the cemetery.

He sits on his heels in front of his empty shrine, follows his breath in meditation until he feels centered. Does a few karate exercises, careful with his feet so as not to tear the tatami mats. Then goes to the kitchen to make tea.

He takes his tea at the low table in the six mat room, idly looking over the pamphlet of sutras given him at the Zen temple. Reads the first one and suddenly recognizes it, though in California they had recited it in English. It is the Heart Sutra, *han ya ha ra mi ta shin gyō*. He reads the pronunciations aloud. He will be able to chant it with the others next time. Then he finds the other one, he has heard that one only the once, but it sings itself to him as he reads, *za zen wa san*. He will practice them, be right there come Tuesday morning.

He gives these sutras nearly an hour, then takes up the book on swordsmanship. He follows the pictures of an old swordsman in a sequence of positions and attitudes, tries to imagine the movements between them. Difficult. It will have to wait. He trades that one for the one on karate, uses his character dictionary to discover the meanings of the names of the exercises, makes notes. No one in his karate classes in America had seemed to know the meanings or think them to have any importance. For them, he thinks, it was all about fighting, not at all about character. He has the first few memorized in less than an hour.

He again looks out over the moat, slides the window open. The day is moist, still, already warm. He hears the mallard hen chuckling, but can't see her or the drake. He hears distant traffic, but sees no cars other than one taxi parked on the stones, waiting under the shrine's high arch. He is going to enjoy his Saturdays for sure.

ち

He has cycled to the Marunaka supermarket, has a basketful of
stores, fresh and frozen. He is on the second floor looking at
school supplies, has selected an elementary school character
workbook. He sees that brushes, inks, other accessories for the
practice of Japanese calligraphy are sold right there, not as art
supplies but for school, right along with notebooks and pencils.
He is tempted, but has no idea what he would need to start.

At that moment Terayama appears at his side. He wears
street clothes, a sportcoat, a blue shirt buttoned to the throat. The
man's timing is impeccable. Too exact to be accidental.

Do you practice calligraphy? he asks.

No, but I would like to. I was taught only to write the
characters with a pen or pencil.

Terayama looks over the selection, picks out a brush, a box
with the word *suzuri* on it in Japanese phonetics, a bottle of ink
and a small black stick of something and a packet of plain paper.
He puts these into West's basket. Then he finds a felt cloth, a metal
bar about a foot long, then rummages around in the texts and
workbooks.

Nothing here any good, he mutters. He picks out another
packet of paper and another bottle of ink.

This will do for a start. Let's go to your apartment.

They go to the front, West cashes out, they split the packages between the baskets of their two bicycles and head for Hachiman Shrine.

In the apartment West goes to the kitchen with the groceries, Terayama goes to the six-mat room with the calligraphy supplies. He has the table set up for brushwriting when West enters a few minutes later.

I need a small cup of plain water, Terayama says.

Yes, Sensei.

He goes and fills a teacup with water, returns. Terayama sits at the table on his heels, eyes closed. He has poured a small amount of ink into a black, rectangular stone and is holding a black stick about three inches long. He pours a small amount of the water in with the ink, starts stirring it with the black stick.

And begins to speak quietly, explaining that the black stick is dry ink, that it is best to make the ink by grinding the stick in the stone with water and not to use the ink from the bottle, but it takes a long time to do that, so he is half-doing it. He tells West to sit and to take over the grinding of the ink. He tells him to look into the ink, to watch the black and the way other colors from the room shine in the black, to empty his mind into the black and the colors shining in it.

When he sees that West is doing this correctly he unwraps the brush and dips the hairs into the cup of water. He explains that the hairs of the brush must always come straight from the base to the tip, never be allowed to twist. When all is ready he opens a packet of paper and spreads it in front of him on the black felt mat and uses the metal bar as a paperweight at the top and dips the brush into the ink and draws it back, he explains, from the sea, the deep end of the stone, onto the land, the shallow, flat surface of it. Always keep the hairs straight. Now shape the point. Then he stops talking and writes *i ro ha*, the first three Japanese phonetic symbols, on the sheet, lays it aside, takes another and writes *ni ho he*, the next three, and continues to write the entire forty-eight symbols three at a time to a page. Then,

Here, you try, he says, and rises and places West before the felt mat and adjusts his posture and his grip on the brush and West writes *i ro ha*, copying Terayama's version as closely as he can. Terayama adjusts his grip, shows him how to move, how not to move the wrist or the fingers but arm and body, the point of the brush always to the northwest, the next attempt looks a bit better.

An hour of this passes as no time. Ink has to be added from the bottle. Then Terayama resumes the seat and writes *ichi ni san shi* on a new sheet, then the rest of the numbers in Chinese characters up to ten and then one sheet with the characters for a hundred and for a thousand and for ten-thousand. He then seats West again and helps him to copy his originals. By the third or fourth try he says that they don't look too bad. Then announces that he is hungry and shows West how to clean the brush and the inkstone. When all is clean and dry he carefully arranges the brush and other materials on the pine plank of the shrine alcove to present a display of them.

You may want a scroll for this shrine, he says, but these will do for now.

West cooks, chicken and some noodles and seaweed. Terayama refuses this, takes out his packet of nuts and nettles. As they eat Terayama tells him where to buy a good copy book for calligraphy.

You can start with these examples of mine, but you will need many more. Kampo-soshi is a good example for beginners. And of course eventually you will need more brushes and a better inkstone and better inks, but these things will do for now.

West knows he has started on a joyous lifetime path.

You know that I don't live in Takamatsu, Terayama says.

No, Sensei, I didn't know that.

Yes, I live in Zentsuji. I come to Takamatsu by train each

Saturday to teach the sword class.

So you stayed over to meet me at the ferry.

Yes.

That means that sword class is today, doesn't it?

Yes. Come and watch. I will write the address for you. And please, don't worry. The taxi won't take you past History Street. One time was enough.

Pardon? Enough for what?

For your training.

With this, his last word other than Sayonara at the door, Terayama leaves him.

The class is in an old wooden building across from a bus depot. Half a dozen men in their odd, skirt-like uniforms sit on their heels on the polished pine floor, sheathed swords pointing back from their left sides. The room is virtually silent, only street noises, mainly from the buses. He too sits on his heels by the door at the back of the room. Terayama withdraws into a tattered tatami room to change.

Older men, generally. Hirano is among them, the youngest at perhaps forty. Most have their backs to him. When one or another of them executes a turn that lets him see a face it is completely impassive. The scent of cloves, faint, somehow calming, vies with the diesel stink of the buses. The movements are silent, graceful, smooth and elegant, each man moving in his own time. Slow, as they draw the sword and rise from sitting position, then a sudden slash. The only sound is a menacing *whoosh* as an overhead cut splits the air. Then another sudden move as the sword flashes into the sheath, followed by a slow, slow descent back into a kneeling position. Each man seems to be practicing a different variation on the theme.

Terayama appears in the same sort of uniform, kneels, bows to his sword and inserts it into his belt. He does a few stretches, a few draws and sheathings. Then he goes to the front and faces the rest of them. He reaches down between his knees to flick the wide skirts of his uniform out side to side, sits on his heels. All the rest do the same. Not a word is spoken as they go through their bows, or when the master performs an exercise while they watch. Then he shouts something, perhaps the number of the exercise, and all the others shout a brief response before proceeding to duplicate his actions. West sits enthralled through the whole two hours of it, forgetting the pain in his legs, forgetting the roar and stink of the buses, forgetting everything. It is the most elegant and beautiful martial art he has ever seen.

り

The summer ends in long rains followed by dense fog on the mountain above the cemetery, reminding him of old ink paintings. He never misses morning meditation at the Zendo, never misses a sword or karate class. He has bought a fine inkstone and a large stick of ink, some other brushes, a handsome lacquered paperweight, and writes for at least an hour every workday, many hours on the weekends. The new inkstone is in an elegant oiled teak box, so it takes pride of place in the shrine next to his sword. He still has no Buddha for it, no scroll.

Terayama often visits before sword class on Saturdays, corrects his calligraphy, writes fresh samples for him, more complicated characters now, most of them to do with Buddhism. He treasures these afternoon visits, though he worries that he doesn't understand the reason for them. Terayama has taken him under his wing, he is kind and generous with his time and knowledge. Why? When will the bill come due?

In the karate class he has been given a brown belt in formal testing, does well enough in the exercises patterns called kata, but has still to win a match in the sparring against the higher-ranked students. He understands the way it's done, the key is never to lose concentration, a special, relaxed sort of concentration, and to see when his opponent loses it. But understanding this is a far cry from actually winning a match.

Hirano says that it is like the Zen meditation, exactly the same. West has yet to experience it as such.

The sword class is a joy. It is a style of swordsmanship called Iaidō, Being in Harmony Way. He has come to draw and sheathe smoothly and without flaw, though still not as quickly as Hirano or the others. He has learned to move his body in harmony with the movement of the sword, which he knows is the first step to Being in Harmony. He has memorized the first set of exercises, the Shoden, Outer Tradition. He watches the older men practicing the intermediate and advanced exercises, but does not yet know enough to see the differences other than in the forms. Terayama nevertheless seems pleased with his progress.

At the Zen temple in the pre-dawn he has now completely memorized the first and last sutras, but still must read the second one. He has no idea how this meditation connects to karate sparring, tries not to worry about it. The days after meditation are always quiet and happy and nothing goes wrong with them. He often strolls through Hachiman Shrine's park, feeling a vague sadness as the plum trees there lose their leaves, as the cats beneath the shrine play less, huddle more. Late at night when the trains have stopped running and there is no more sound of traffic, he hears a plaintive melody played on a bamboo flute and has twice run down the stairs to try to spot the source of it, so far with no success. He tells himself that he is not lonely, but on these occasions he thinks he might be lying.

His work at Yamazaki Industries follows a routine. Now he always brings his Japanese grammar and dictionaries to the office with him, and some text or another of his own to study or translate, so the hours there are not wasted. He has the occasional piece of Yamazaki work to translate, too, and is deep into one when Mr. Ikeda clears his throat and says, Excuse me please, Mr. West. Can you tell me what means Tacking down the Dateline?

He hands his copy of *Time* across the desk. West reads the

article. It is an interview with a rich businessman, also a famous yachtsman, who now in his later years is suffering from Alzheimer's disease. He describes his episodes of falling into and out of dementia as being like Tacking down the Dateline.

Do you know what Tacking means? he asks.

Well, in my dictionary it has several meanings. But when you come to Tack Down, it means to fasten a carpet to the floor.

Right. No, in this case, it means sailing into the wind on zigzag courses.

Yes. I understand that one.

And the Down here only means Southward.

I see.

Now, you know about the International Dateline?

Yes. It is a longitudinal line in the Pacific exactly opposite to the Greenwich Meridian. It is today on one side, tomorrow on the other.

Yes, or yesterday on one side and tomorrow on the other. Anyway, if you are sailing a zigzag course and you are using a clock and a sextant to find your position, you have to know what day it is to read the position of the sun and stars. If you are crossing the Dateline every time you tack, you can't know for sure what day it is. So you are lost for much of the time.

Ah, now I understand. Then he says, Only in years instead of days. So he felt he was lost in time.

Exactly, West says. That's it exactly.

And he thinks, that's how it is for me, too, only in centuries. A Zen temple from the Muromachi period, a post-war apartment building, a 19th century office and a 21st century computer shop, all in a given day.

This is in November, when half the people on the streets wear surgical masks and huddle low on their bicycles against the cutting wind. West often forgets that he is foreign, a gaijin, is often surprised to see a western face in the mirror. So on such days he too wears a mask, though he has not yet caught a cold. He enjoys the anonymity of it, often wears sunglasses on these days and sometimes a beret. Thus the gaijin disappears. Apart from his size, taller than most Japanese, he feels himself to be passing entirely as one of them.

ぬ

New Year's Eve at the Hachiman Shrine. Throngs of people at midnight, strikingly quiet and serious, pay their respects and draw their fortunes for the coming year from a booth opened next to the main building. The fortune comes on a small piece of paper handed out by a beautiful young Shinto priestess, based on a number derived from a throw of sticks from a wooden cylinder. It lists lucky and unlucky days, directions, elements, numbers. Over all the great bell at the cemetery tolls slowly, lending the entire affair a solemn tone completely in contrast to Times Square. He mingles for a while, then watches from his window. It takes more than an hour for the bell to ring its hundred and eight strokes, but the people continue to cross the bridge over the moat, back and forth, for hours after that. He has a drink to everyone's health and well being and goes to bed about three.

On the second day of the new year he takes an inventory of his stores. He has a good supply of rice, instant noodles and two huge bottles of sakê laid in, but little more than soy sauce to put on the rice and noodles. The kitchen presents a bleak prospect. He cycles out to the Marunaka and finds it closed. He knows of course that Yamazaki Industries shuts down for the first week of the year, but no one has warned him that all the rest of Japan simply closes up for that period too. Streets deserted, not a shop or a restaurant open. He cycles the city searching for a mom and pop store, somewhere they might live in the back or upstairs and be persuaded to sell him a few bits of this and that.

He does finally find a place, mainly a tobacco stand, in the Ta-machi. A tiny, ancient woman, permanently bent from years of work in rice fields, sits huddled by a portable gas heater in her open-front shop. It is near sunset, the light coming through the translucent plastic of the street covering dull and eerie. He wheels the bike up to her counter, kicks the stand and wishes her a Happy New Year. She says nothing but smiles softly, her tiny eyes glittering up as if she is happy to see him. He points to cans of tuna and mackerel, a quart of milk, some chocolate digestive biscuits. It all makes him very happy. He smiles at her, gives her a bill. She gives him change and gives him what he takes to be a smile. She never speaks. He doesn't know if it is that she can't believe a gaijin can understand Japanese or that she is a mute. Still, the feeling is very warm, as if she's an old friend or a loving aunt. No idea if it is mutual, but he thinks it is. When he gets the stuff into the bike's basket, mounts and kicks the stand, he waves and smiles and says Happy New Year again. He thinks he sees that ghost of a smile and perhaps a tiny wave in return.

It is quite dark by the time he gets home. As he is mounting the stairs with his bag of stores he sees a great rarity on the bridge over the moat. A tall, slim gaijin girl with long blond hair walks her bicycle toward the shrine. In the months he has spent in Takamatsu he has seen few other foreigners—a Catholic priest, a few seamen from the repair facilities in Marugame, the pair of tall blond Mormon boys on their bicycles plying the missionary trade—but this is the first foreign female he has seen there.

He wants to ask her up for a cup of sakê for auld lang syne, but there is something about her bearing that puts him off, head sunk on her chest, shoulders slumped. He takes his stuff upstairs, packs it away in the kitchen, pours himself a Suntory Old whiskey and goes to his window overlooking the shrine.

Strong streetlights illuminate the bridge and the moat and a few dim ones line the walkway to the main hall and fairly strong lights glow in the eaves of the building itself. He can't tell if she is there at first because she is so still, but he spots her at last, sitting in a lump on one of the stone benches next to the path, just out of the pool of light from the shrine building. It is cold out there, a faint but cutting north wind, damp and sea-smelling for the lack of traffic, though still carrying some scent of the trains. Not a kindly breeze.

He is torn. In the end he guesses he is just too curious to leave it alone, but there are surely other motives as well. He puts on his coat and shoes and goes quietly down the staircase.

There is a way to sneak onto the grounds he thinks, but he doesn't try, just moves quietly and slowly across the center of the bridge, softly between the guardian archers in their houses, down the center of the wide stone walkway. She doesn't budge. He watches her every second. He feels fairly sure she is crying. As he gets closer, he hears an inconsolable mewing sound. The cats under the shrine catch his attention. They huddle together miserably in the cold. Some of the sound comes from where she is sitting. He sees that she has a kitten in her lap, barely the size of her hand. He walks up, says hello, very softly.

She doesn't look up. It's terrible how they treat their animals, she says. American accent, California or the midwest or just television-generated. The kitten is sick, has left patches of diarrhea stain on her light trench coat. It sucks on her finger, mewing in sad futility. One rear leg is extended at a bad angle. It looks mangy.

Terrible, how they treat their animals, she says again.

Seems out of character, he says.

Do you think so? It seems quite in character to me.

She sniffs. A tear falls, hitting the kitten's eye. It mews

louder.

Look, my apartment's right over there, he says. Bring the kitten up. We'll give him some milk. I'll rig a litter box.

No, she says, I'm going to keep him myself.

Of course. Just to fix him up a little for the trip to your place. He's certainly not happy now.

She thinks about it for a moment, then rises without a word and starts walking back toward the moat. He follows. She is about his height, even bent over the kitten in her arms. When they've crossed the bridge he realizes she's left her bicycle behind, which means she is taking up his offer. He leads her then to the stairs, to his door. She sits down on the wooden step in the vestibule to pull off her boots with one hand, unwilling to let go of the cat.

He puts milk in a saucer and hands it to her. She puts the cat on the kitchen table in front of it, starts him off with a few drops on a fingertip. He gets the idea instantly, lapping and mewing alternately. West gets the impression that the cat's voice is getting stronger with each milliliter. He finds a box of calligraphy paper, some old practice sheets of it he is going to throw away. He shreds the paper into the box and puts it in the vestibule.

He asks if she would like a whiskey, sakê, coffee, tea. She would like a whiskey and coffee, if it isn't too much trouble. It isn't. She puts the saucer and the kitten on the floor and goes to clean her coat and herself. The cat explores, finds the box and has foul-smelling diarrhea in it, scratches away at the shreds of paper while balancing on its one good rear leg. The right one still drags badly as he goes back to the milk. His eyelids are stuck together with mucous. He yowls miserably when West cleans them, but blinks to show some fine green color under. He has only half a tail, typical of Japanese cats. West puts him down, washes his hands and finishes filtering the coffee.

Her name is Carrie Barr, she is from San Diego via the University of Hawaii. She teaches English as a Second Language for a private language school in the Kawara-machi. Very pretty in that healthy, California way, twenty-two. First job. First time out of the States, if you count Hawaii as part of the States. He gets her to agree to tuna and noodles, his own Italian style sauce instead of the stuff in the package. Wine instead of sakê. The kitten has filled up on milk, burped, begged, and is asleep in a ball but for the dangling leg, purring like a chain saw on her lap. He cooks. They drink whiskey.

She eats voraciously, having been caught as he has by the general New Year's shutdown. They eat with forks instead of chopsticks, as he's guessed from her comments about Japan that she wants reminders of home. He wants to know what has gone so sour that she is sitting at the shrine alone in the dark and the cold, but the mood is good for the moment and he doesn't want to risk it.

They move to the front room for coffee and more whiskey. The cat protests at first, but a bite of tuna, another ounce of milk and another messy visit to the paper box put him back to sleep. They sit on cushions by the cleared calligraphy table. That mysterious plaintive bamboo flute echoes in the hollowed out streets.

I fell in love, of course, she says, trying for a world-weary tone. You've noticed how some Japanese men are so damned handsome, like bullfighters or Flamenco dancers? I thought it was mutual. Then this damned New Years' holiday. He had to go with his family to Kobê. To meet his fiancée's family.

What do you want to do now? he asks her.

Die, of course. No. Go home, I guess. He was the only thing I liked about Japan. Now he's gone . . . .

Tears. Tissues. Apologies. Another whiskey. Worries him a little; the bottle is low and you can't buy it out of the machines.

In the end he moves the table and lays out the futon for her and the cat there in the front room, sets up his own in the other. He gives her a paternal goodnight kiss once she is tucked in. The cat is tangled in her hair, purring so loudly he can't see how she is actually going to be able to sleep. It looks as if the whiskey had arranged for that, however, even before he slides the door closed.

There is no writhing with frustrated desire, but there is confusion. He has not thought about women for over a year, his focus on his studies having been so intense. She is a beauty and sweet in her manner and suddenly seems to him a real danger. He wants no diversions. The night looms long. He looks forward to the sound of the cemetery bell at six AM.

He gives her coffee in the morning and sees her out, the kitten a bundle in the bosom of her trench coat. Sunny day. He watches from his window as she walks back to the shrine for her bike, straight now, strong mover. She doesn't carry a purse. She has a little trouble pushing the bike over the bridge one-handed, the other securing her kitten. He can make out the shape of the cans of tuna he's given her in the pockets of her coat.

る

He starts backsliding, his concentration begins to fail at meditation, though not too badly at karate or sword classes. He calls to find out how the cat is doing, asks her out for dinners, hangs around the school where she teaches trying to get a glimpse of her. She never wants to talk to him, is barely polite as she refuses every invitation. She is snagged in his mind. He is obsessed with her, pictures of her, fantasies.

His teachers notice, of course. He is ashamed on top of the suffering itself. He tries to drop it, can't. He has lost his way.

She calls him one day a few weeks later to tell him that the cat has died, the mange proved incurable, she is leaving for home. He will never see her again. This doesn't help his spirit at all. Though he misses no sessions he makes no progress, finds himself drifting at meditation, forgetful of characters, hopeless at sparring. The rest of his winter is bleak indeed. He finally catches his cold in late February. He takes a week to shiver and sweat in his futon with the heat up as high as it will go.

In one of his feverish periods of sleep he has a dream. Facing a problem in translation, he goes into the mountains south of town where there is a craft and souvenir shop. He has never been up there in waking life but in the dream he has visited often. There a young man who wears a High School uniform has a room at the right side of the shop, and a girl or woman he has never

47

seen has a similar room at the left end. Their doors face the front, toward the dusty road. They are blue, western-style doors, even though the central part of the building is traditional rural Japanese. He has often consulted with the fellow on language and cultural matters and he has always found him very helpful. With this particular problem it seems he cannot be of any help, and he suggests that West visit the girl at the other end of the shop. West is reluctant to do so. The boy shows him an old brass key. This is the wrong kind, he says. She has the right one. West stands there gazing indecisively at the girl's blue door until he wakes. When he does it is dark and warm and he is damp from sweat but he is no longer sweating.

を

It is the first Monday in March, he has managed to eat, to bathe, to dress. He is thin and weak but thinks he can walk down to the shrine to thank Hachiman-san for an end to his illness. He bows, claps, rings the bell, tosses a coin. Fills himself with gratitude. As he walks back toward the bridge he notices the early buds on the plum trees, tiny, green-wrapped symbols of hope.

At Yamazaki Industries later in the morning everyone welcomes him back, wishes him good health, congratulates him on his recovery. He is sorry, but he is unable to explain a rock star's description in *Time* Magazine of his solos when drugged as Synch-opiated instead of Syncopated. Hirano asks him if he thinks he will be able to attend the karate class this evening. He says he thinks he can. Then he sets himself to correcting the English in a pile of correspondence to an American computer manufacturer.

The afternoon lengthens. West gives up on the correspondence, picks up his copy of the text on swordsmanship and works on his translation of it. Yamazaki emerges from his office, bleary and rumpled as ever, stands uncertainly watching them all and clears his throat. They all look up from their desks.

A week from Saturday, he announces, Yamazaki-kaicho will come to Takamatsu and will give a dinner for all the staff. It will be at six o'clock at the Keio Plaza Hotel. Everyone please come.

There are nods and mutterings of Hai Bucho, arigato gozaimasu. Yamazaki leaves, and all heads bow again to the papers on the desks.

West and Hirano are well down the street toward the karate dojo before Hirano says, That means we will have to leave sword class early next week.

Will Terayama-sensei be angry? West asks.

He will understand, Hirano says.

That evening in karate class he goes through the stretches and calisthenics and kata but has clearly been weakened by his bout with the virus. The teacher excuses him from sparring and he is grateful. He watches the matches with interest, paying great attention to the eyes and the posture of each of the students and guessing at who will win and who will lose. He is wrong most of the time, which makes him wonder if he will ever understand how it's done. The meditation after the sparring is a muddy stream oozing through him and leaves him feeling tired and dull and lonely. He begs off from dinner with Hirano and cycles home in the chill to eat a bowl of reheated rice with some seaweed on it, drinks some sakê.

He wades in the same muddy stream at the Zen temple in the cold morning. He is able to sit in complete stillness but his mind moves, he loses his place in the chanting of the sutras, the day following the meditation lacks the sparkle he remembers from the past. Instead it cowers beneath a gray drizzle. The correspondence he is given to correct at Yamazaki Industries is almost incomprehensible and completely pointless. No one in the office has spoken to him beyond their first good mornings. Just as well. Cycling home with a nasty windblown rain in his face he wonders if he is still sick. If so it is no longer the virus. At home he reads an English paperback mystery. When he wakes the next morning he does no stretches or kata but lies on his futon and lets his mind trace pictures of Carrie Barr and discovers that it is not about her anymore but he cannot find whatever it is about. Whatever it is. Whatever it is it is certainly despair.

On Wednesday night he is able to do the whole karate program, even the sparring, though he loses every match. On Thursday morning he is able to quiet his mind somewhat and can chant all the sutras, but that is all. On Friday he takes his English paperback mystery with him to work and hides surreptitiously in it.

On Saturday morning he is reluctant to rise, resents the tolling of the six o'clock bell. He is apprehensive about the arrival of Terayama, dreads the embarrassment of letting the old man see his desultory calligraphy. Still, knowing it all is inevitable, he drags his sluggish body off the futon and stuffs the bedding haphazardly away in the closet. He showers and dresses and makes tea and hides with it in his English paperback mystery.

In less than an hour West finishes and promptly forgets the ending of the mystery. He lays out the calligraphy things and glances at them now and then in thorough distaste. Terayama actually arrives some two hours later than usual. West is surprised to see him in a blue pinstripe suit, white shirt and red foulard tie.

No calligraphy today, he says. Dress well. We're going on an outing.

West tries to shield the messy futon in the closet from Terayama's view as he seeks out a suit, shirt, tie. He changes quickly in the back room, goes to the mirror in the bathroom to knot his tie, presents himself. Terayama nods. They slip into their shoes and descend to the street, where Terayama hails a cab. Takamatsu Bunka Senta, he tells the driver, and off they go to the city's cultural center.

There Terayama leads him to a side entrance. It's a modern building in Western style but for some classically clean Japanese wood columns and trim. They pass through a lobby and enter an exhibition hall filled with flowers and women hovering over them, butterflies in their bright kimono, a riot of color in the midst of a whisper akin to a quiet stream or waterfall, the flow of feminine Japanese softly spoken.

This is the spring festival of Ikebana, Terayama tells him. Ikebana. Do you know?

Flower arrangement, West says, stating the obvious.

Yes, but more than that. A Zen art. Come, I will show you.

They move slowly down an aisle between the many tables until Terayama finds a particular arrangement to suit the points he wants to make. It is three stems of Bird of Paradise set in a green-gray vase carved from a solid piece of rock and filled with water reflecting and repeating the colors above it in muted tones.

In shapes it is much like our calligraphy, he says, the way the eye must trace the empty lines between the strokes. But in the movement of the colors it is somewhat like your abstract expressionist painting. The other important matter is the sense of the gesture, the feeling that each stem was thrust into place with complete confidence. Can you see that?

I think so, Sensei.

Terayama smiles past him, bows. West turns and looks down and sees a tiny gray-haired woman bowing deeply, wearing a kimono less bright than most he has seen there. The old man introduces her, the head of that school of flower arrangement.

You enjoy the flowers? she asks.

Very much, he says, though Terayama-sensei is just now teaching me about them.

They move on, with Terayama choosing one or another arrangement to study in detail. At the far end of the room he pauses before a spray of cherry blossoms.

You know about the meaning of the cherry blossoms? he asks.

Yes, Sensei. The Samurai and the fleeting nature of life.

More than that, but yes, that.

A woman who appears taller and, though it's hard to tell with the wide obi she wears, slimmer than most of the others, stands in rapt contemplation of the next arrangement. She is in bright kimono and has very straight posture. West observes her in profile, sees a straight nose long for a Japanese, full lips, high cheekbones. She shows no sign that she is aware of being watched. Terayama is between them, seems absorbed in the cherry blossoms.

This one is very good, he says. Whoever did it knows about the sword.

On hearing this the woman turns to him. Sensei, she says. How kind of you to say that.

Terayama looks at her in surprise. She bows. He says, Ah, Hanako-san. I should have known the cherry blossoms were yours. Miss Sakurada, this is West-san, my student.

More bows. West sees her in full face for the first time. It is heart-shaped, fine-featured, large-eyed. The mouth is wide. It is a modern face somehow, does not match the traditional clothing or the mass of black hair pinned high with jeweled combs. He guesses her age as about thirty. He does so by doubling the age she appears to be.

How do you do, Mr. West, she says in British-sounding English. I'm surprised to meet you here, this way. We will meet again soon.

Excuse me, but how is that? he asks in complete bafflement.

I too work for Yamazaki Industries, she says.

West notes that Terayama is not attending to any of this, that he again studies the cherry blossoms, then sends his eyes far across the room. In another moment he turns abruptly and bows to Hanako-san and says that they must move on. She bows, West bows. They leave her.

The rest of their time at the exhibit is spent without words. West simply follows his teacher from table to table as he pauses now and then to examine one particular piece or another. When they have completed their circuit they step back out onto the street, exchange bows.

Sword class tonight, Terayama says. Don't be late.

West promises that he will not, and in the event is a few minutes early and finds himself practicing with solid con-centration, his mind entirely clear and his movements light and coordinated. His overhead cuts split the air with magical vibration, his sword slides in and out of the sheath as of its own volition. He knows that Terayama has noticed because he teaches him a new exercise. He sleeps well for the first time in many days, and gives Sunday joyfully to his calligraphy, applying to his characters what he has learned from the flowers. He briefly wonders whether this revival is because of the flowers or because of his time with Terayama's powerful spirit or because he has met Miss Hanako Sakurada.

For whatever the reason the ensuing week flows smoothly from the meditation hall to the karate dojo to his desk at Yamazaki Industries. His calligraphy pours out in shining streams of black onto the perfect white paper void. He seems to have lost all awareness of himself in his every action. On Wednesday night he fails again to win a match sparring but for the first time manages not to lose one. This is the true life of Zen, he reflects, even knowing that this very reflection is a flaw and not minding that and forgetting it instantly. How beautiful is spring.

わ

He and Hirano enter the hotel, find the banquet room and leave their shoes and join the gathering, everyone still standing, in the tatami-floored banquet room. All men, Yamazaki and Ikeda from the office, no Miss Oka. The rest West has never before seen. Perhaps thirty of them all told. The only women there are the waitresses in flowery kimono.

Until the arrival of Sakurada Hanako, with three westerners in tow.

He hardly recognizes this woman he'd met a week before, who had worn traditional kimono and whose hair had risen in a luxuriant array above her head, so black its highlights were almost blue and adorned with glittering sticks and combs. Now her hair is cut barely to shoulder length, bangs cover her forehead, ends curve outward to one side in a fashionable wave. She is dressed in a pale serge three-piece suit, a white shirt with flowing collar and a dark blue cravat. Her make-up is subtle but for the bright lipstick.

The three American men she ushers in wear rumpled business suits, only one of them, older than the other two, wears a tie. The younger ones have that truculence often seen among computer whizzes. All three shamble. She glides. She is vivacious with them, attentive, a mixture of Japanese deference and western flirting.

Yamazaki-bucho raises his left wrist, stares at his huge gold watch until he is noticed, begins to usher everyone to their places, where they stand behind the cushions placed around the U-shaped arrangement of long tables. The seating order appears to be strict and according somehow to rank, except that West finds himself led to the highest seat on the left arm of the U and the three other gaijin are placed in the three highest on the right. Hanako takes the fourth. She has to put a hand on the arm of the nearest of the three to quiet him when two Japanese men enter and stand behind their places at the center table. Hirano slips in line to stand next to West.

The younger of the two wears a perfectly tailored pinstripe business suit. The older—much older—wears a very formal, dark brown kimono, white split-toed socks on his feet. He appears abstracted, perhaps even ill. His few wisps of thin gray hair are carefully plastered to his translucent skull. All bow as the younger mutters a phrase, perhaps of welcome. Then all sit. The flowery waitresses bustle in with carafes of sakê and thimble-sized cups on trays. Conversation resumes. Laughter. Cigarettes are lit. After a few moments of this silence falls again as the younger of the two at the head of the table stands and speaks.

West can understand the opening phrases of welcome, bows from his seat with the others as the old man, Yamazaki-kaicho, founder and president of the company, is introduced. But after that he watches and listens only to Hanako, who appears to have dropped into a kind of trance, her eyes closed, hands folded in her lap, she is translating every word for the three gaijin with whom she sits.

First these gaijin are introduced, Smith, Jones, Brown, West forgets the names as soon as they are spoken. They are from a company in California considering a major purchase of the products of Yamazaki Industries. He hears her whispered instruction to them to make small bows from where they sit.

While they do so, West forces himself to shift his attention to the speaker, another Yamazaki, brother, it seems, to his boss. He then hears his name, his description as the first foreigner to be employed at Yamazaki Industries, Japan. He bows from his seat before Hanako has caught up with the translation, mutters arigato as he does so. He thinks this a small victory, then realizes it may well have been just the opposite, at worst the relinquishing of a secret, at least the embarrassment of having been seen to be a show-off.

He returns his attention to Hanako, listens to her translation rather than to the speech itself. He finds himself fascinated by the complete impassivity of her face, the immobility of her body. He hears her speaking in her perfect British English, the voice mellifluous, the phrasing a little fragmented by the reversals of grammar required in translating from the Japanese, but it still seems impossible that she is here in the flesh and not being broadcast straight from the U.N. This self-effacement of the woman who had just moments before vivaciously entertained her western visitors disconcerts him, even somehow frightens him in its unnatural self-mastery.

After much about the fine character of the Yamazaki employees, their great loyalty and selfless service, and the virtues of the Smith Jones Brown Company of California and the great friendship between the U.S. and Japan, the company applauds itself. A response is called for from Smith-Jones-Brown. The older man speaks in Midwestern English. With not a single change in her position or demeanor but only a slight raising of her voice and its pitch changed upward, Hanako translates this simultaneously into Japanese. This seems to flow more easily for her, the fragmentation gone now. What is said is banal and cagey in either language. West catches her rendering certain phrases more politely than Smith-Jones-Brown has intended them.

Applause follows this speech and when it has settled he

hears his name both as West from Hanako and Uesto from the speaker and it's clearly time for him to make his own speech. He decides to do this in English through Hanako, though it seems a bit late to cover his earlier gaffe. Proud and grateful, etcetera. Brief. Her translation seems accurate. He bows and mouths an arigato to her, but she is still in her trance.

More applause, more sakê. The food arrives. It is lively for a time, the food sashimi, red snappers curved artfully on beds of ice, gasping still as they are flayed and eaten. Smith-Jones-Brown are appalled, eat the pickled vegetables and other odds and ends, refuse the fish. West too is repulsed by the cruelty, but eats the fish with great pleasure in its freshness even before mere freshness. It touches him with some atavistic energy he'd never known in himself before. He looks across at Hanako to see if she is eating the fish or is too polite to do so in front of her charges. He sees that she nibbles on vegetables only and avoids the stare of the dying beast. She avoids his glance too. He turns to speak to Hirano.

So, Yamazaki-kaicho founded the company, did he?

Yes. At first it was not about computers, but his eldest son, the one seated on his right, talked him into it.

And the son's title, what is it?

Yamazaki-sakaicho, I think. Vice president.

As for Yamazaki-bucho, is he the youngest brother?

No. The youngest is the one who taught you karate in San Francisco.

They pour sakê for one another. Kampai. Empty cup. It occurs to West that this can have more than one significance. In Zen you empty the cup of the mind.

There is a short period after the fish have died at last and are removed when some of the men at the tables stand and move about to pour sakê for one another. A middle-management type kneels between Hirano and West, pours for them. Hirano pours for him. In badly accented English he asks West, Are you happy at Yamazaki Industries?

Yes, West says, it is very interesting.

Do you know computers?

No, but I'm learning.

There is much to learn.

Indeed there is.

Then a few fast words to Hirano which West can't follow though he hears the word gaijin in it. After a brief negative from Hirano the fellow withdraws with a very curt bow.

There is the tinking of a chopstick on porcelain, a brief speech of exhortation, a last toast and a loud Banzai from all but the gaijin group. Yamazaki-kaicho is helped to his feet by Yamazaki-bucho. Yamazaki-sakaicho leads the old man out. All rise and make final bows, then begin drifting toward the foyer, where shoes are sorted and donned. West watches Hanako, vivacious again, chatting and smiling and no doubt apologizing for the inconvenience of Japanese customs as she guides her three shambling clowns to the doorway, helps them find their shoes. Then she is gone.

The fellow who poured sakê for us, Hirano tells him. He wanted to know if we would go out drinking with him and Yamazaki-bucho. I told him no. Is that all right?

Yes, I think. Will the bucho mind?

No. It was just to be polite.

Good. I don't want to drink any more tonight.

Me too. Sleep well.

Yes. Sleep well.

He has some trouble reconciling the sakê with the bicycle but works it out finally, though he takes a wrong turn and has to walk the bike through a neon street of bars and drunks and past a girlie show with a pair of 1930s pinstriped gangsters out front trying to look as dangerous as they can manage. They see the sword case slung across his back and turn away.

After that he is back on the Marugame-machi and knows his way and cycles home with Sakurada Hanako in kimono with her flowers and in her fashionable suit and salon hairdo with her foreign visitors and these pictures add to the confusion left over from the sakê. By the time he has racked the bicycle and bowed across the moat to the shrine and trudged up the stairs and unlocked his door and removed his shoes and arranged his futon all has resolved itself into exhaustion and he sleeps instantly.

か

Today her hair falls long and frames her face in black parentheses and if she wears makeup it is invisible. She wears a bulky sweater and dark slacks and has a large bag slung across the back of her chair as she leans forward to cradle her coffee cup in both hands. Her hands are without rings and seem tiny and fragile and perfectly smooth and beautiful. She avoids West's eyes, stares into the blackness in her cup. They are the only customers in the coffeehouse this early afternoon. The room is dim and the walls and ceiling and all the furnishings are veneered in shiny black formica.

Your studies. Karate and the sword, isn't it? And you go to meditation at the Zen temple.

Yes. And Terayama-sensei is teaching me calligraphy.

That's good. Something fierce and something gentle, and the Zen to integrate it all. I too study karate, she says in English. Not just tea and flowers and haiku. And I studied archery when I was in college. Not very ladylike.

And English, he says. How is it you speak it so well?

My father worked for the diplomatic service and I lived a long time in London. I went back there as an interpreter after college.

An amazing talent, that simultaneous translation.

It's a trick, but yes, I suppose it's a talent as well. A gift.

But now you're back here and working for the Yamazaki. How did that come about?

I only work for them on occasions like the other night. Mostly I study the arts. But I want to hear about you. Why you want to study these things.

I met a young Japanese, who turned out to be Yamazaki Takeshi. He taught karate near the University in San Francisco. I joined his class. He set me onto Zen as well.

He looks down at his cup, the black liquid reflecting black surfaces reflecting black liquid. He is not sure he should say more. Then he has to tell her.

There was something in the karate and the Zen I found compelling. Just moments, instants. Yamazaki-sensei told me that those moments meant I should come here to study, to immerse myself. That became my dream.

He feels he has embarrassed himself by saying so much. He raises his eyes to see how she has taken it. Sees nothing. Goes ahead.

So I went through graduate school in Japanese language and humanities. When I finished my degree, Yamazaki-sensei arranged this job for me with his family's company. So now I'm living that dream. Looking for what lies behind those moments.

She seems to sense his embarrassment. But the job, she says. How do you find the work?

He is grateful for this less personal question. Not very demanding, that's true. Sometimes I think it's not very important, either.

She looks at him with what seems to be a new intensity, her eyes now are black, entirely black, in a face ghostly pale in that light and disembodied in the curves of black hair and everything in the room surrounding that face black, a palpable emptiness.

When her words come they are widely spaced, her voice sounding disembodied too, heard not in the room but inside him.

He knows he is experiencing some kind of lapse of consciousness but can do nothing about it.

Do you know the history of the Senkyo Sect? she asks.

He shakes his head, cannot speak.

The young man behind the counter noisily turns a page of his sports magazine. The sound intervenes in a way that allows West to return to this coffeehouse and this time and to see and hear normally again.

Her natural voice returns. It is very old, she says, and there are many secrets. It is not for outsiders.

I certainly am one of those, he says.

Perhaps for now. One day you will be told what you need to know.

Now I am intrigued, he says with a smile.

You are meant to be, she says.

He expects her to smile back but she does not. He loses his smile and searches her face for a meaning she seems to expect him to see behind her words. He finds a mask there, a Noh mask, revealing nothing but its perfect beauty. She suddenly is older, not the thirty he has thought her to be but truly old, much older than he, an ancient, timeless mystery.

She pushes her cup aside, draws her purse onto her lap, pushes her chair back. I must go, she says abruptly. We will meet again.

She rises and slings her bag over a shoulder. He stands too and they bow. Before he can say Sayonara she turns to leave and then, without looking back, says, When Terayama-sensei considers you ready, you will be given a Special Assignment. I can tell you no more than that.

He watches her walk out the door and away to disappear among the women shopping in the Marugame-machi as if she were one of them and not the ancient, timeless mystery he has just seen. He pays the young man behind his black formica counter and leaves to walk back to Yamazaki Industries.

There he cannot escape from his reverie, the words Special Assignment repeat themselves, inviting speculation he dare not afford them. He stares at a few papers on his desk but sees only her face, her hands. He intently recalls her every word and motion, willing his memory to raise every nuance of that strange meeting, to fill in the gaps where he knows his consciousness has failed him. All he finds new is the impression that their meeting has not been accidental, that she has watched and waited for him.

He toys with his dictionaries and reads again the brief introduction to his book on Senkyo style Karate. Not much there either, just that the school was founded by a 17th century monk on Mount Koya named Senkyo, who considered the art essential to his sect of Buddhism. He reads it again and actually writes out a translation, but really that is all it has to say. He closes the book and closes his eyes and rubs them and looks across his desk at Mr. Ikeda's baldness and beyond to the elegant calligraphy of the document hung there incongruously in its polished wood frame on the roughly plastered wall. He supposes it is the company's motto or charter or license, something like that, but he isn't sure. He tries to read it but can't at that distance, wonders if he could, even if he got up and walked over there, dictionary in hand. He tries instead simply to imagine what it says, what perhaps he might want it to say. What he thinks he wants it to say is that Sakurada Hanako has intended at their meeting to give him a warning, though what her warning might mean he knows that framed sheet of calligraphy could not tell him.

よ

At the Zen temple the next morning samadhi comes even as the priest chants the last phrase of the Heart Sutra, so that he and time both disappear entirely. When the break comes he remains seated, just rocks his body, twists his head. The second meditation is the same, no dreams, no illusions. At the end he feels as fresh as the new day dawning over Takamatsu.

He meditates again in his apartment after work and the effect is perhaps not as complete, but he is surprised to find himself so peaceful. The question of the Special Assignment banished from his mind, he stretches and exercises and sits to his brushes and papers and inkstone and has a vision of Hanako as Kanon, Goddess of Mercy, she protecting him from harm. He gives no more thought to her warning, simply knows that he will know what he needs to know when he needs to know it. He writes Kanon many times, the characters meaning Contemplate the Sound.

Through the rest of March and into April his studies go smoothly and well, he learns all of the first set of sword exercises and actually wins one sparring match in karate. There is still little work for him at Yamazaki Industries, so his list of memorized characters expands at a steady rate. He can read almost all of the Japanese newspapers now, and understands most of what is said to him in direct conversation. The slang he hears spoken on the street still eludes him, but he doesn't worry about it. It will come. He will know what he needs to know when he needs to know it. He thinks of Hanako often but with no anxiety or longing. She will see him when she wants to see him.

In April he receives a letter from her. It is on fine Katsu paper and written beautifully with a thin brush in a subtle gray ink. It begins with a haiku about cherry blossoms, then invites him to view them at Ritsurin Park on the following Saturday. He finds himself somewhat uneasy about this, as if it presents a difficult challenge rather than a simple pleasure. He feels certain that this is a famous haiku, though he doesn't recognize it, so he will not have to spend hours with his dictionaries and his small brush to compose two seven-syllable lines to link to her haiku. Still, he must practice writing an acceptance of her invitation and confirmation of the time and place. This takes him hours anyway until he thinks it doesn't look too bad, though he knows his writing lacks anything like the elegance of her hand. The return address on her envelope is in Kobê, across half the Inland Sea from Takamatsu. Full of surprises, this woman.

た

He sees her standing at the end of a row of trees. The trees are twisted and bent into amazing giant bonsai. She is dressed in the style of an office lady, white blouse, black skirt, flat-heeled black shoes, black leather shoulder bag. Her hair is long again today and straight, with bangs just skimming the frames of large tinted glasses. He recognizes her immediately. People walking under the trees on their way into or out of the park seem not to notice her. One or two glance at West, who wears a pair of khaki pants, a white shirt with no tie, a light sportscoat. I am gaijin after all, he notes. It's not how I'm dressed.

When he reaches her they bow formally and wish one another good day.

Let us speak in English while we're here, she says. She does not smile. This is the chestnut grove for which the park is named, she continues. Very beautiful, aren't they?

Yes, very beautiful and impressive.

We will cross some arched bridges across ponds. Some have carp and others lotuses.

The lotus pond is quiet and deeply peaceful this bright, still day. The carp flash in the sun in their carefully-bred goldfish patterns, then hover under the shadow of their bridge like ordinary, hungry fish. Pausing to watch them, West glances at Hanako, is surprised to find her looking at him. He waits before giving her the smile he thinks would be appropriate. She does not smile but searches his eyes and so he does not smile and searches her eyes too until a group of people approach the bridge, chatting and lugging picnic baskets and sakê jugs and other picnic paraphernalia.

They follow that group at a distance and a much slower pace. Some distance away he sees a cloud of shimmering pink and white hanging in a grove of trees. They walk toward this without words.

As they near the grove West sees that these are the cherry blossoms and that many are falling as a slight breeze rises, and that under them are picnickers, eating and drinking and singing loudly. Hanako gradually guides him down a smaller path through the trees, deeper into the grove where there are fewer revelers and then none. West looks up at the trees and the blossoms which swirl and glint with the clear sky behind them and fall softly on their heads and shoulders and carpet the ground in subtle shades. Neither speaks. They do not touch. West finds himself unaccountably close to tears.

Their way eventually leads them out of the grove and onto a wider path. Beyond yet another pond the tiled roofs of traditional buildings appear. They amble toward them. One, smaller and off to one side, is of rough wood and wattling and has a roof thatched rather than tiled.

It is a teahouse, she tells him. I will make tea for you there.

They rinse their hands at a natural stone basin set among a bed of ferns shaded by tall pines. She removes her sunglasses and tucks them into her shoulder bag. They leave their shoes on the wetted stones of the foyer, and bow to enter through the low doorway. They kneel on the tatami and contemplate a sprig of cherry blossoms in a raku vase and a scroll in the shrine which reads only Quietude.

The attendant, an older woman in a brown kimono, bows

and brings in an iron pot of water, places it on a hot bed of charcoal in a stone-bordered depression in the floor. She bows again and withdraws and then brings two raku bowls with a bamboo whisk and ladle and a small jar of powdered tea.

As for sweets, will you want them? she asks Hanako in a whisper of Japanese.

No, thank you, Hanako whispers back. The woman bows again and Hanako and West bow to her as she again withdraws.

Traditional tea then, the bubbling of the pot, the incense scent of the charcoal, the cascade of the water as she ladles it into the raku bowl, the perfectly-modulated accelerando and retardando of the whisk as she whips the tea into a froth, her every movement smooth and graceful and as ritualized as kata. The moss-like surface of the froth, the rich-earth smell and faintly bitter taste of the tea. He sips and she sips and he sips until they have emptied the bowls. She wipes the rim of hers with her thumb and index finger and rotates the bowl. He does the same and passes it to her across the tatami between them.

Another? she asks.

He declines.

She cleans and tidies the tea things with the same graceful and efficient motions. When all is arranged she turns to face him, both of them still folded into kneeling position, and bows to him and he bows to her and suddenly she grasps his face and kisses him, they kiss, a long open tongue-spinning kiss, when she withdraws he fears unconsciousness.

As they are leaving the park she speaks in English whenever people are near, is silent when they are alone. When she speaks it is in the sing-song tone of a tour guide, telling him that the park once belonged the Matsudaira family, that it went public in eighteen seventy-something, that all the hills and ponds are artificial. When they reach Chuo Avenue she bows as he thanks her, they say Sayonara and walk off in opposite directions.

れ

Two days later he receives a postcard with a haiku written in her hand:

Cherry blossom cloud
Glowing brightly in the sun;
Lotuses open.

The card itself is of a heavy handmade paper with the pale outlines of cherry blossoms behind the calligraphy. The postmark again is Kobê. It bears no other message, no signature.

It seems obvious to him that she expects two seven-syllable lines in return, so he starts with a pencil, scratching out every other sound until at last he has something he thinks might work. He grinds ink and wets a small brush and practices over and over until he thinks it is not too bad.

Fecundity of Lotus;
What else may open this spring?

He writes a final version on a similar card, handmade but with no cherry blossoms, addresses it, puts it in the post with a shrug. He knows it cannot be good Japanese poetry, but at least he thinks it parses. He then returns to his writing table and resumes work on his lesson for Terayama's next visit. It is a four-character phrase reading Sword Cuts Illusory Lightning. Roughly. He is finding Terayama's assignments increasingly difficult to translate, let alone to write well. Today is Tuesday. He will have four more days to work on it. Hundreds and hundreds of copies. He'll have it eventually, every curve of black and shape of white exactly as the example.

Well. Close, anyway.

そ

It is Saturday morning and raining heavily and when he answers the knock on his door he expects to see Terayama but instead faces Sakurada Hanako. She wears a long brown trench coat and rubber boots and a plastic scarf covers her hair and she carries a bunch of wet fresh flowers and a huge plastic bag.

Terayama-sensei could not come, she says. He asked me to teach you calligraphy today.

He bows and invites her in. She sits on the wood floor of the vestibule with her feet on the concrete lower floor and removes her boots and a pair of white socks and the plastic scarf and puts the socks and the scarf in her plastic bag. Her hair is as it was the last time he saw her, long and straight and with bangs. She twists to place her bare feet on the wood. Her feet are slim and her toes are long and perfect and their nails silver-polished. She slips gracefully into formal kneeling position. He drops into that position facing her.

Welcome, he says in formal Japanese, bowing.

Forgive my arrival, she answers formally, bowing also.

They pause there, he remembering their kiss and wondering if it would now be repeated. She stirs to rise and he knows it will not be and they stand and she unbuttons her coat and he takes it from her and hangs it on one of the hooks to one side of the vestibule. She is wearing a black pullover and leotard.

Would you have coffee? he asks. Or tea?

Yes, coffee please. But please let me arrange these flowers first.

They go to the kitchen and there she rummages through cabinets until she finds a ceramic vase she considers suitable, Then she withdraws to the six-mat room. He starts the flame under the kettle. When she returns and they are seated and sipping their coffee he asks,

As for Terayama-sensei, is he ill?

Yes, perhaps.

Will he teach the sword this evening?

Perhaps not. There will be practice, but no lessons.

I understand. Thank you.

He finds some chocolate biscuits and serves the coffee and they drink the coffee and nibble at the biscuits.

Your table, is it ready for calligraphy? she asks after a silent time.

Yes, it is.

Well, thank you. This was delicious. Shall we begin?

Yes.

They go into the six-mat room and sit at the table. She examines Terayama's samples and his copies while he grinds ink on the stone. She watches him grind the ink for a while, not speaking. When he has a quantity of rich dense ink she says that it is enough. She resumes her examination of the samples and the copies. It is the text Sword Cuts Illusory Lightning.

These are good copies. But of course they do not have the energy of Terayama-sensei's originals.

I understand.

She gathers all the papers and tucks them under the table out of sight. Write them for me now, from memory, she says.

He does one so.

Close your eyes now and remember how it felt when you watched Sensei write them.

He tries to do this, sitting with eyes tight shut and watching the shriveled old man as he writes them and tries to remember how it felt and then knows.

Write it again, that way, she says.

He does so. As he does, the brush feels the same as the sword.

Much, much better, she says.

She rises and goes to the vestibule and delves into her huge plastic bag and returns with a plastic wrapped roll of papers. This is fine paper, about as wide as the practice sheets are long and then four or five times their length. He has never before written on paper of this sort. She shows him how to do it, but writes nothing herself. She tells him to write the four characters on the fine paper, larger, on the vertical. His first attempt is not successful, he knows, the change in scale and format leading to poor alignment and variations in the size of the characters. She takes that one and rolls it up and gives him another sheet and he writes it again. A little better. Twice more and the ink is gone and she tells him to grind more. While he does that she rises and goes to the kitchen and after a while returns with a pot of tea and two small cups on a tray and they sip tea as he continues to grind ink. The great bell tolls twelve times. When it has finished she takes the tea things away and returns and says The ink is ready now, write the phrase again.

He feels settled and focused and having visualized the phrase as he wishes to write it many times as he has been grinding he knows how to do it exactly and he does and it feels wonderful, as if she had taken his hand with the brush in it and has written it for him.

Beautiful, she says quietly. Yes, that is truly yours. May I keep it?

Of course.

She takes a push pin out of her plastic bag and goes to his shrine alcove and pins it there where there is no scroll and sits formally before it and watches it for several minutes.

Then returns to the table and asks him, do you want to write some more, or should we stop now? I have brought some lunch.

So he cleans the brushes and the inkstone and clears the table while she takes her plastic bag to the kitchen and prepares their lunch. It is a kind of sushi not molded but loose and scattered and mixed, served in lacquered boxes. She has heated sakê and serves that with the food and they pour for each other from the small bottle into their tiny cups and sip as they eat. When they have finished he says It was delicious, thank you. She says It was nothing. There are a few drops of sakê left and they sit sipping that. The rain starts again and they watch it as it beats against the sliding glass doors and whips the distant pines on the hill beyond the JNR and the Buddhist cemetery.

She rises then and clears the table, telling him to stay seated, enjoy the rain. He hears the water run as she cleans the lunch things and then hears the water heater in the bathroom start and then the shower running and doesn't know what to think, sits listening to his apartment and watching the rain and there is a humming in him much the same as fear though it isn't that. After a time he hears the bathroom door and the sliding door to the four- and a half-mat room and then the sliding door to the closet there where he keeps the futon and the quilts, and he knows. He rises when all the sounds have stopped and opens the sliding door between the six-mat room and the four- and a half-mat room and sees her lying on the futon wearing a thin cotton sleeping robe. He removes his black cotton karate uniform and kneels beside the futon and they kiss long and slow and tongue spinning and he is rock hard and her nipples push rock hard through the thin cotton and she smells faintly of flowers and strongly of her wetness and then she opens her robe and presents him with the beauty of herself and then they are together, long and slow and then fast and then fiercely and he knows his life has changed forever.

〜

The great bell tolls six times.

You have missed sword class for the first time.

Yes.

It is all right. Terayama-sensei will not be teaching.

Yes.

We must write some more.

Really?

Yes. It is important.

All right.

He rises and puts on his black karate uniform and goes to the six-mat room and sets the table for calligraphy while she in her light cotton sleeping robe goes to the kitchen and makes tea. He is grinding ink when she brings the tea and serves it.

That is enough, she says. We can use bottled ink from now. I will write first.

She kneels and pours tea and he moves aside to let her have the writing place at the table. She wets the brush and on a practice sheet writes *sokushin-jōbutsu*.

Copy this, she tells him. It means To become a Buddha in this Living Body.

Yes.

She moves aside to let him write, sips her tea as she watches. The four characters are not difficult in block script. As he writes she begins to speak.

Kukai brought the Shingon sect of Buddhism from China to Japan. Shingon doctrine holds that a living human being can come to know the Ultimate Reality while still living in this world. This is what is called Nirvana. To attain Nirvana in this life requires not only complete immersion in meditation, but also many other practices. One of them is to follow a strict diet, mainly of certain nuts, completely avoiding grains.

That is what Terayama-sensei is doing, isn't it?

You have noticed. Yes. He has been working on it for some years, gradually. Now he grows weak from it. He should not be teaching and working. He should be sitting still and cared for in a monastery. I will be your calligraphy teacher from now on.

And the sword?

That too. He will appoint a successor.

I see.

Do you have this memorized? she asks after he has written several copies.

Yes.

So now, let me write something else.

They trade places. She wets the brush and takes a fresh sheet and writes *Senkyō-ryu Den*. He knows that this means The Tradition of the Senkyo Sect.

Now you write it, she says, and they trade places again, and again she speaks as he writes.

Senkyo founded the sect on Mount Koya in the seventeenth century. He was then of the Shingon sect. But while Senkyo still held with the idea of *sokushin-jōbutsu*, he thought the martial arts were necessary to its other practices, and that Zen offered a better way to meditate. No more gods or demons, no more secret words or postures. So he broke away and made the new sect.

She pauses here, looks at what he's written. Again, she

says. The *den* character is too small with the others.

Yes, Sensei, he says, and lays out a new sheet.

She seems to hesitate, to ponder.

One of the practices they took from Shingon was the making of Living Buddhas. Do you know what that means?

No.

It means that certain monks and priests would follow the diet, even more intently than the rest, and would determine that they would persist in this until they died. Certain barks and leaves that they added to this diet, coupled with deep meditation, would begin to dry up their bodies from within and gradually preserve them. Near the end they would cease to eat altogether and go into a cave to sit in deep meditation. Eventually they would die, but in a state of deep samadhi and with their bodies entirely dried and preserved.

You mean mummified, he says.

Yes. They become mummies.

Why?

To attain Nirvana. But also to prove to later monks and priests and anyone who would later see their mummies the power of discipline and meditation. Thus they remain exemplary teachers and inspire others even beyond death. Hence the term Living Buddha.

I see. Did many priests do this?

No, not many. Perhaps one in any generation. There is more.

Yes. Please continue.

In the nineteenth century, the Meiji government issued the Separation Edicts, by which Buddhism was persecuted. Many religious artifacts were destroyed, and monks over eighteen and under forty-five years old were drafted into the Imperial army. Seeing this happen to temples in or near the cities, The abbot of the Senkyo temple took a few younger and older monks and fled to the Tosa mountain here on Shikoku Island. There they built another Senkyo temple, in complete secrecy, and returned to Mount Koya.

Then, during the wars in China and Mongolia and the Pacific War, Buddhist monks were again forced into service by the National Mobilization Law. The military government even used the temple grounds for training them as soldiers. A few protested against this. Very few. The punishment for this was often harsh, with the monks imprisoned or set to slave labor in factories, the temples ransacked or even burned. The Senkyo Sect did not protest, but withdrew even further into the mountains near Mount Koya, living in huts and without a temple as such. By then they had hidden their dozen or so mummies in sealed caves far from roads or paths.

But one young monk was angry with the abbot of the time, disagreed with him about the war, felt that the Senkyo Sect, having skills in the martial arts, should serve the military government. His name was Bankyo, which means Guardian of the Doctrine. Some guardian. He left the sect and went to a garrison, where he told the officers where the monks were hiding and where the mummies were hidden. There was a raid. The abbot of that time led a charge against the army. They had only swords and wooden staves against rifles, a machine gun, hand grenades. The abbot was the first to die, and all but a few of the monks were killed. All of the mummies were burned. But one mummy was not there. That one mummy was Senkyo-kai himself. Its location was known only to the abbot in any given generation, and he was dead. It was not there, because it had been taken to the secret temple in the Tosa mountains during Meiji, almost a century before. The monk Bankyo did not know of this temple, so the mummy of Senkyo-kai was saved. The only one remaining.

After the war Bankyo went to America, to California, where today he makes films in which the women are dismembered and murdered after having sex. Not with special effects, but really dismembered and murdered, on film. There seems to be a large market for this in Japan. We hear that he is very successful.

She has finished. He sits watching her. She is in stillness as she kneels formally, her gaze lowered. He tries to see beneath her beauty and to comprehend what she has just said. In the distance he hears the recorded, high-pitched voice of a woman blaring from a sound truck, touting a Pachinko parlor. He sees that the rain has stopped and that a cloud shrouds the cemetery and the slope above it.

That is truly damned evil, he says. Incomprehensible. And he was once a monk.

Yes.

Then after a few moments, he asks, Has this do with my Special Assignment?

Perhaps, she says, not looking at him. I think it may.

I see.

He wants to ask more but she rises and goes to the bath and he hears the shower again and then after a while he hears the tap of heels on the kitchen floor and then the hiss of the gas of the stove and sees the light burning on the other side of the mottled glass door. It is nearly dark. She is cooking something.

He does not look into the kitchen but goes through the four- and a half-mat room and into the bath and showers, shaves, then puts on his own light cotton sleeping robe, straightens the futon. It is fully dark now. He closes the shoji screen over his window to the shrine and turns on a small lamp. Then he goes to the kitchen.

She is frying bread and eggs and wears black stiletto heels and a black thong and a thin gold chain around her waist and that is all. She does not look up from her cooking but asks Do you have white wine?

No, only red. His throat is thick.

Please pour some and set this table.

Yes.

It is difficult for him to eat slowly and to sip the wine rather than gulp it and his eyes throughout stay fixed on her exquisite breasts and when she has finished and stands he stands too and embraces her from behind and there is the hard place where it belongs and they leave the dinner mess and go to the futon in the four- and a half-mat room and this time it is wild and then slow and complex and has many novel variations and he is altered again, changed yet again forever.

ね

He awakens alone well before dawn, first to a feeling of loss, and then of amazement. It really happened. She is real. I am real. He indulges in remembered flashes and is incredulous despite his certainty of their reality. He rises and stretches and goes to the bath in the dark, showers himself into consciousness.

She has left the mess in the kitchen. He smiles. He clears space to make coffee, toast. In the six-mat room there is bland early gray. There is still dense fog over the cemetery now, even shrouding the JNR. The bell has not yet rung its six. His calligraphy no longer hangs in the shrine alcove. He smiles again.

Over coffee and toast he reviews her history of the Senkyo Sect, the mummies, the traitor. His Special Assignment will have to do with that. He will be asked or ordered to go to California and stop Bankyo's murderous pornography. What else could it be? He will have to pose as one of the monk's rich American clients, and will have to kill him.

And somehow get away with it and never tell anyone who sent him.

A terrible honor. He has never been so honored. He will have to redouble his efforts with both sword and fist, become good enough and strong enough and fast enough and smart enough. This thought weakens and terrifies him.

The tolling of the great bell rouses him. No rattle of the

train on a Sunday. He cleans the kitchen, prepares his calligraphy table, exercises, sits to meditate. When that is over the fog has cleared and the light is golden as he sits to grind ink. He copies earlier assignments from Terayama, trying to remember how it felt when the old man wrote them, until he can try them from that memory. He thinks they look better.

Assigned to wreak havoc on Bankyo. Redouble your efforts.

He writes all day.

On Tuesday he redoubles his efforts in morning meditation at the temple. He is not sure how he is supposed to do this, as meditation is thoroughly passive. He tries nevertheless, and then thinks later that he reached samadhi despite doing so.

That night he dreams again of the souvenir shop. The schoolboy again tells him that he must ask the woman behind the other door. Only she has the right key. This time he dares to do so. He knocks and the door opens of itself. Behind it stands a bent old woman. She smiles faintly and silently offers him a key. He takes it. The metal is so hot it burns his hand and he drops it in the dust.

On Wednesday he receives another postcard. Her haiku reads,

> *Evening rain in spring*
> *Bringing both joy and sorrow;*
> *Hearts dry come morning.*

How can he add two sevens to that?
Redouble your efforts.

> *Faced with both joy and sorrow,*
> *Hearts are both full and empty.*

That night at karate class he redoubles his efforts. He wins no matches. Thursday morning he redoubles his efforts at meditation and fails to reach his trance-like state. On Friday he receives another postcard from her, no haiku, just the note, Calligraphy on Sunday.

He spends Saturday at calligraphy redoubling his efforts and he is able to write block script well, but anything else he tries fails. When it is time to cycle to sword class he is intently focused and ready to redouble his efforts.

な

Or so he thinks. The new teacher is Nomura-sensei, a stout, hard, scar-faced man in his fifties. West has seen him at every class, in the first row. He is very fast with the sword, and his cuts don't whisper through the air, they scream. Now he screams at West.

As for the last class, you were not here!

Yes, Sensei. Terayama-sensei sent word . . .

That matters not! You will not miss class again!

Yes, Sensei.

The man is on him through every exercise. No! Your wrist! No! Your knee! When the class is finally over he is soaked in sweat. Sword class is somewhere he definitely can benefit from redoubling his efforts.

As he and Hirano are folding their uniforms, Hirano speaks to him in English. He was hard on you tonight, he says, but he will not always be like that.

I won't miss class again.

I think that would be good. Do you want to go for dinner?

No, thank you. I'm too tired.

He is almost too weak in the knees to cycle home. As he passes Hachiman's arch he sees a few people on the grounds, mere shadows in the sparse lights along the walkway to the shrine, it is a soft cool evening. He parks his bike in the rack under the shed and walks on shaking legs to the stairs and up to his apartment. He is dispirited and exhausted.

She is there. She is damp from the bath and her cotton sleeping robe is nearly transparent with the moisture. She silently hands him a dark whiskey even before he has removed his shoes.

Sunday, you said, I thought.

For calligraphy. Tonight, for you.

Thank you.

I have brought dinner.

Thank you.

The bath is hot.

Thank you.

He undresses and stacks his clothes askew over his sword case and uniform bag and stumbles into the bath room. Showers, shampoos, rinses. Slides with his whiskey into the steaming tub. Sips. Sweats. Almost sleeps.

She enters with a huge towel. Takes his glass, puts it in a corner on the tiles.

You should come out now, she tells him.

Yes.

Too much and you will be faint.

Yes.

He stands and she helps him get his legs over the high side of the tub and wraps him in the huge towel and rubs him briskly. Guides him to the four- and a half-mat room. Helps him into his sleeping robe. Goes back for his glass, guides him to the kitchen, seats him at the table. Adds whiskey to his drink.

Dinner soon, she says. I have brought tempura domburi.

Thank you.

As for Nomura-sensei, he is a harsh teacher, isn't he?

You know him?

Yes.

Yes. He is harsh.

You have worked very hard all week, haven't you.

Yes.

Too hard.

Yes.

Dinner now.

With the bowl of rice and shrimp and other fried things she brings stemmed glasses and a bottle of French white. It is chilled and dry and now he gradually revives as the hot food and the cold wine overtake the languor of the whiskey and the bath. Her robe has dried, has opened to reveal some thigh, some curve of breast. She smiles as she sees him noticing this.

Tonight I will do everything, she says.

And so she does. Everything he has ever imagined and much he has never imagined even in wild erotic dreams. Afterward he weeps and then sleeps as if dead. When he wakes he realizes she is cleaved to him tighter than he is to his own body. He doesn't stir though he would like to find a way to look at her sleeping but he can see only her hand on his chest and the mass of black black hair, nothing more. He thinks he will weep again but when he closes his eyes to stop the tears he sleeps again.

When he wakes the next time in full light she is not there and he panics for a moment and then hears the ting of a cup from the kitchen and knows she is still with him. He rises and finds his sleeping robe and goes to the bath. When he has showered and shaved she is still in her sleeping robe and waiting for him at the calligraphy table. Fresh flowers are in a new, more elegant vase in the shrine.

She pours his tea as he enters. She has already ground ink and has been writing. Small writing, winding its way down the page, sinuous vines free of trellises. He watches her write as he sips tea and eats a biscuit. Her face is serene but entirely focused on the page. Her movement of the brush is alternately light and forceful, not at all rushed but, he suddenly realizes, extremely fast.

You cannot copy these, she says. This is woman's hand. But you should learn how to read it.

She finishes a sheet and passes it over to him. He can make out some of it, very cursive Chinese characters mixed with phonetic symbols he knows but finds hard to distinguish in this form. It is better just to look at the page as a whole, as an ink rendering of a hanging garden. They spend an hour as she traces the lines for him, writes them in a more standard style. He thinks he is beginning to understand it.

Now I will write some phrases for you to copy, she says.

The first one reads Form is Exactly Emptiness, which he knows from chanting it at the temple and has written often before. He tells her this.

Do you understand it? she asks.

No.

No one is meant to understand it, I think. Through meditation, it is something that can only be experienced.

I see.

And through writing it many times, perhaps.

Have you had the experience of it?

Perhaps.

She rises and stands aside and has him write it many times. She occasionally makes a suggestion. He redoubles his efforts.

That is why the week made you so tired, she says.

Yes.

How do you call it?

Redoubling my efforts.

Hmm. Not that way. Let us meditate for a while. Then watch me again.

They sit side by side facing his shrine alcove with nothing in it. He is intensely aware of her, her scent, her breathing. But after a while her stillness laves him and his mind quiets and he attends to his own breath and he disappears and she has disappeared and he silently chants the phrase Form is Exactly Emptiness with each exhalation and soon even that goes away. When at last she stirs he is slow to join her back in that other time-place.

They straighten knees and rub feet and flex toes. Hers so graceful. When she stands she takes some karate stances and turns them left and right to bring back the circulation in her legs. He rises and does the same. Without speaking she sits at the writing table and grinds a little more ink and wets the brush with great delicacy. At exactly the moment she touches brush to paper she disappears, he can see some wraith-like spirit but nothing of her body, the brush moving powered by nothing but spirit, she writes the four characters in a single load of ink and when she places the brush back on its rest her body is here again in all its serene beauty.

Now you, she says, and makes room for him.

And so he sits to write and writes the phrase then perhaps a hundred times with his eyes on the blank page and then lifts the brush and inks it and writes the phrase with brush and ink on paper and while it's a good copy he does not do what she did he does not disappear and he knows it.

Again, she says.

He writes it again.

Again, she says.

He writes it again.

Again. Again. Again.

You are harsher than Nomura-sensei, he says.

Again, she says.

The noon bell tolls and he has written it ten thousand times and he has still not disappeared.

Chant with the bell, she says.

He chants. Form is Exactly Emptiness. Form is Exactly Emptiness. Form is Exactly Emptiness.

Write it again, she says when the twelfth rich tolling has faded.

He writes it again, empty with hopelessness. And as he does so he disappears. When he returns he looks to see her watching him, calm as the Buddha himself.

It is the same with the sword and the karate, she says. No redoubling. No efforts.

Yes.

Good. Clean this up now, and I will make our lunch.

After lunch they return to the futon and she says, It is the same with this, too.

Neither of them does anything, yet it happens between them, he feels some nameless force moving his body and hers and it is the same but entirely different and again he knows he has been changed forever. Again. Yet again.

When he wakes she lies beside him propped on an elbow, watching him. She smiles a thin smile.

You watch me, he says. Why?

I'm waiting for you to ask a question.

He discovers that the question has been forming in his mind, he can't help it, but he knows he must not ask it. He can see that she sees in him the question fully formed, even though he has not quite formed it for himself yet and even if he ever forms it for himself he will never ask it.

She simply answers it.

I learned it all from reading the tantric sutras, she says. In some sects in those days they thought that one could reach Enlightenment through the joining of yin and yang, and established sexual practices for the purpose. A priest named Tachikawa formed such a sect here in Japan, but it was declared a heresy. I read everything, and don't worry about heresies. As to your other question. No, never before, never with anyone else.

He breaks from her eyes. Is this part of the Senkyo doc-trine? he asks.

No. But neither is it forbidden. It is only forbidden to become attached to it.

He closes his eyes and stretches and tries to understand what she has told him, what it means to him, what it says about her. He has started with one question, now faces a hundred new ones. He sighs, puts them all aside, drifts. She lies back beside him, allows him to drift.

After a while he washes up on a bleak shore, a gray place somewhere, he thinks, in the future.

I think I know what I will be asked to do, he says. For my Special Assignment.

He feels her tensing where their arms touch, then forcing herself to relax.

What is it, do you think? she says.

I will be told to kill Bankyo in California.

That is what you think?

Yes. Because he will be on guard against a Japanese, but not a gaijin.

You feel certain of this?

Do you think I should not be certain?

She doesn't answer, turns away.

I think you should not say this to anyone else.

I understand.

Do you know if this will be my assignment? he asks her.

No, she says abruptly, still looking away.

Does it seem likely to you?

After a pause, still looking away, she says, Perhaps.

They get up and dress in their robes and he goes to the six-mat room while she goes to the kitchen to make tea. He looks out to the cemetery and the green hills beyond and is certain of it, even if she will say nothing, and he is surprised to discover that he is not at all afraid.

ち

All through May and June she comes to him late on Saturdays, leaves him late on Sundays. She always brings fresh flowers and teaches him calligraphy and many other things. Many other things. She has become not only his teacher and his lover but also his muse and inspiration. His studies go well, he feels strong and fast and clear.

Near the end of June she tells him that she will not come to him the following week. She has duties in Kobê related to the Tanabata festival.

I must attend a meeting at our temple there, she tells him. It is a large gathering of calligraphers. A writing competition.

I see. May I attend it too?

Her eyes widen in sudden alarm. Oh no, she says. It would not be right.

Why not?

It is only for members of the temple. No observers.

I see.

But of course he does not see exactly. He does see that she is not telling him everything and it worries him. As she is leaving him in the dark of Monday morning she whispers Don't worry. I will see you soon afterward.

Terayama arrives at his door on the next Saturday

morning, carrying a package wrapped in cloth of indigo print. He seems smaller than West remembers and very brown, but straight-backed and still moving well. He is dressed in his priest's robes.

Good morning, West-san. Today is Tanabata festival. We will write together.

West has already begun writing, so the table is ready. Will you have tea? he asks.

Yes. But only this tea, Terayama says, withdrawing a small lacquered cylinder from his voluminous sleeve. West takes the tea to the kitchen, puts on the kettle. Terayama seats himself at the writing table and examines Hanako's examples and the sheets West has just written. He makes no comment, but stares at each page intently, comparing one to the next, making three piles, moving pieces from one stack to the next, back and forth. West watches this curiously from the kitchen door.

The kettle finally boils. He pours the water from the kettle to the pot. Terayama's tea smells dangerous and disgusting. He puts the pot on the tray with only one cup.

Smells bad, doesn't it? Terayama says bowing. It is only for me, my strange diet. He looks back at West's writing. It is much better, West-san. She is a good teacher, ne?

Thank you, Sensei. Yes, she is a very good teacher.

All in a very academic style, very formal.

Yes, Sensei.

Show me some earlier work.

Yes, Sensei.

West goes to the cabinet where he keeps the pieces Hanako has praised, those he'd written when he'd disappeared. Those she had written using his hand.

These pieces are on good paper and fully a meter long, so Terayama makes no piles this time but rises from the table and unrolls them on the tatami mats. There are six of them. He spreads them out, then steps back and looks at them one by one, stepping from left to right, right to left, back and forth several times.

Hah, these are very good, West-san. Beautiful, truly.

Thank you, Sensei.

All right. We will write big like this today, but in a different style.

They roll up West's pieces and put them away. Then Terayama kneels and opens his cloth package and brings out a box. In the box are two brushes, about twice the size of the largest one West has. They are three or four centimeters in diameter at the base of their soft white hairs and have gracefully turned wooden handles. They are identical except for the color of the woods, one nearly black, the other reddish.

This one is for you, he says, bowing and holding the reddish one in two hands above his head. West takes it in his two hands and bows with the brush above his head and says Thank you, Sensei. This is too rich a gift.

It is nothing.

So they arrange the table for writing on long sheets and take turns, Terayama writing first, West copying his examples. The characters have a wild sort of beauty, and reflect their mood. A feeling of joy, pleasure. Fun. Just fun. They write sheet after sheet, West no longer copying Terayama's characters but mimicking his motion, his grunts and shouts, his breathing, his laughter.

See, West-san? A different style altogether.

They laugh. Fall down with laughter. Cry tears of laughter. When he can laugh no more he asks Sensei, What do these say?

They are lines from a drinking poem by Rihaku. Very funny.

I offer sakê to bright moon.
Moon already has no excuse for drinking.
I sing. Crazy drunk moon spins.

They laugh some more.

West lays out a large felt pad on the floor and they spread the sheets on it six at a time. Can you pick out yours from mine, West-san?

Perhaps. He puts those he thinks he's written to the left, those he thinks are Terayama's to the right. Some he simply remembers. Others he can only judge by the energy of the strokes, certain that the stronger ones must be his teacher's.

Is this correct? he asks when he has finished.

I have no idea, the old man says, and again they break into laughter. Then Terayama says, You must be hungry. The Noon bell rang at least an hour ago.

They sit at the kitchen table to eat, West a heated package of Cup Noodle and Terayama leaves and nuts from the bag in his sleeve. West now knows the reason for the old man's strange diet, wants to ask him how he feels, what he thinks about this thing he is doing. He is not sure how to say anything about it. Terayama saves him the trouble.

Hanako-san told you of the reason for my diet, he says.

Yes, Sensei.

She explained that this diet is necessary.

Yes, Sensei. But Sensei, doesn't it leave you weak?

Yes, lately my body is weakened and getting very stiff. That is why I no longer teach the sword. This writing today was very hard, and I am tired now. But oh, wasn't it a great pleasure?

They laugh again, but quietly.

Now I must go and rest. I will observe the sword class tonight. Nomura-sensei is a good teacher, neh?

Yes, Sensei.

A bit harsh, ne?

Yes, Sensei.

Never mind. Persevere.

Yes, Sensei.

West sees him out the door with the conventional bows and phrases. Even knowing that he will see him later that very day, he feels a terrible sense of loss.

む

Again, at the O-Bon festival in August, she cannot come to him. Neither it seems can Terayama. He buys a decent summer kimono and a pair of wooden sandals in the afternoon and then in the evening goes out to see the parade of bands and synchronized dancers and traditional musicians as they pass Hachiman Street on their way up Chuo Avenue and is stirred by the old music and the odd sense of impending death so celebrated. He is amused to see Hirano and Yamazaki and even Mr. Ikeda in their summer robes and wooden sandals dancing in a group representing Yamazaki Industries. He is relieved that he had not been invited, or worse instructed, to join them.

Moon-viewing in September, Sports Day in October, Seven- Five- and Three-Year- Olds' Day in November. Her absence on holidays has become a pattern, less disturbing for that. It remains something of a mystery nevertheless. She will give no explanation beyond Duties at the Temple. Each of these festivals involves some activity at the shrine, so he spends much time during them watching the passing scene beneath his window over the moat. Seven-Five-Three is the most delightful, the children in their bright kimonos repressing their mischievous delight for the formal demands of the occasion.

But now it is winter and the shortened days are often gray and there is much fog and rain. He knows she will not be with him for the New Year, Duties at the Temple, and dreads the emptiness of that week. At least this year he will stock up and be prepared.

う

He receives another card from her. This time it is in an envelope.

Shrine's moat sheathed in ice.
Winter Solstice darkens hearts.
Below, water flows.

And then a note. Take the last train to Imabara after your sword class. Sit in the First Class car.

It would be easy to answer the note. Writing two lines of seven syllables he thinks would not. He sits to his table, grinds some ink and wets a small brush. It comes as if it had already been written.

From the wellspring does it flow,
Through the ice to empty sky.

Despite his curiosity and anticipation he disappears with every sword exercise. Nomura-sensei notices, singles him out for instruction. Through this he is present, but when the teacher goes on to another student he soon disappears again, knowing that he is performing even these new and more difficult exercises perfectly. When he has changed and packed his bag and cased his sword he cycles the cold distance to the train station completely in the present, no past, no future.

There he racks his bicycle with hundreds of others, goes in and buys his First Class ticket to Imabara, not letting any questions arise concerning this mysterious trip. The train won't leave for over an hour, so he crosses the square south of the station and walks to a restaurant where they grill meats. The place is warm and crowded and smells wonderful. He has *Jingiskan*, lamb named after Genghis Khan. He drinks a small bottle of sakê.

When it is nearly train time he walks back to the station, buys a newspaper, finds his platform. The train is already there. He takes a seat near the back of the First class car on the nearly empty train. He has packed his shaving kit and a change of linens just in case.

The train leaves on time. There is nothing to see out the window, so he opens the newspaper and soon wishes he had brought his dictionary. There is little foreign news, lots about skiing and skating in the sports section. This is a semi-express train, barely slowing until it reaches Sakaide, where it makes its first stop. There the two businessmen who had taken seats near the front get off. He has the car to himself. The First Class car is expensive and never crowded.

In a few minutes the train stops again, in Marugame. He gives up on the newspaper, dozes. One elderly man in a well-cut suit gets aboard, sees West, sighs, takes a seat well to the front. He gets off at the next stop, Tadotsu, the junction where this eastbound track intersects with the southbound trains for Kochi.

He hears the sliding door open behind him. Smells strong perfume, opens his eyes, careful not to turn his head. She suddenly drops her black leather bag on the floor, sits next to him and puts her cold hand on his. She wears a short fur coat, tight jeans tucked into high black boots with spike heels, heavy makeup, bright red lipstick, black eye liner, false lashes, blue shadow, a huge and obvious henna wig. She meets his eyes and smiles just a little.

Do I look like an American whore? she asks in English.

Yes.

Good. I meant to. It's a disguise.

Successful.

Thank you.

Why?

Because we are going to a hot springs hotel. I will only wear this to check in. It would not be necessary in Tokyo or Osaka, but way out here it is.

I see.

The train stops only at the major stations, Kanonji, Kawanoe, Iyomishima, Nihama, Saijo, Toyo. It is after midnight when they get off at Imabara, take a cab. They cuddle and giggle and speak only in English on the drive to the spa, with the driver often glancing in the mirror. It's a long drive.

When they reach the hotel she puts on a large pair of red-tinted glasses. She has reserved the room in his name. The night clerk at the desk checks them in with averted eyes. The bellman leads them to their room without once looking at them.

They sit to remove their shoes in the rudimentary vestibule. Beyond a sliding door is a six-mat tatami room. Two futons are already laid out, with sleeping robes neatly folded on the pillows. There is a mini-bar. To the left is a western style door to a private toilet. She points to it.

Let me get out of this costume, she says.

It takes her a while. He goes to the mini-bar and opens a miniature of Suntory Old, pours it into a glass, listens to water running, stopping, running again. Sips the whiskey and looks at his reflection in the window. Waits.

She emerges at last wrapped in a white bath towel, looking herself again. She unfolds one of the sleeping robes, turns modestly to put it on, takes the towel back to the bathroom. When she returns she says in Japanese, Change now into your robe. We will go down to the baths a few minutes apart. They are separate for men and women. Wear the slippers you will find in the box in the vestibule.

Yes.

He begins to undress. She bows slightly, says Until later, and leaves.

The bath is beautiful, natural stone, pine slatted floors, water shrouded in fog. No one is there. He strips and sits on a pine stool and washes himself at a bamboo spigot, pours the hot water over himself from a pine bucket. Eases himself slowly into the steaming pool, stunned at first by the heat, then gradually losing all tension in his body. He thinks he will disappear into the water, but he does not.

He dreams again of the mountain souvenir shop. The two blue doors are padlocked. He considers going in through the central traditional doors but does not. He waits in confusion. A waterfall appears among the rocks and trees above the shop. It has a peaceful sound. He walks around the left side of the building and there follows a path that twists upward in the general direction of the waterfall. Small stone figures line the path at irregular intervals. Strange animals, a froglike creature, an elongated fox, a tiny ogre. He hears a croak. A bark. A gurgling laugh. Rounding a large mossy boulder he sees a glittering flash of light. It proves to be water in the pond beneath the fall. In a grotto under the waterfall a monk sits in the Lotus position. An ornate robe is draped over his head and shoulders and he seems to be grinning.

Time ends. He thinks he may die and is untroubled by the thought. Hanako's face floats up out of the water. You must leave now, it says, though with neither sound nor movement of her mouth. You must leave now.

It seems impossible, yet he manages to move one arm,

then the other. He finally is able to sit on the wet-polished stone of the rim, then rolls his legs up and out of the water. It takes him a long time to rise and walk unsteadily to where he has left his towels and robe. He dries himself and wraps himself in the robe and walks zombie-like to the shoe box and steps into his slippers and makes his way back to the room.

The room is dim, only a small paper-shaded lamp burns on the floor near the futon. She kneels in meditation facing the dun plastered wall, neither turns nor speaks. He quietly crosses the room and kneels beside her and silently chants the Heart Sutra, then disappears. Time ends.

She softly touches his hand and he returns and they remove their robes and lie on the futon.

What happened in the bath? she asks him.

I had a dream. Then time ended and I thought I might die, but you came and told me to leave.

That is good. Was it a good dream?

No. The doors were locked. But there was a pool and a waterfall and a priest in a red robe.

That is good too. Now we will do something good here, neh?

ぬ

She doesn't wear the wig or the spike heels in the morning. Her black hair hangs straight and long and she wears dark slacks and training shoes. They do not stop at the desk, but go straight to a waiting cab, take it to the station in Imabara. There they check their bags in the left luggage office, take another cab to a small, nameless village where they rent bicycles. The day is brisk, calm and clear. It is hilly and dusty on the dirt road, from which they see a beautiful temple. Cycling is hard on the climbs, exhilarating on the downhills.

He has never been here, but they come to a road that is level and curving and feels familiar to him. They ride now at a leisurely pace, enjoying the cool shade of the forest lining the road. There is no car traffic, only a few people on bicycles, one party of hikers with wooden sticks, traditionally dressed as pilgrims, going their way.

After a time they round a bend and he sees the souvenir shop. There is a large old tree in front of it, and a rack with several bicycles. It is not exactly the same as in his dream; there are two log benches that were not there, and the two flanking doors are not western style, but have blue canvas half-curtains. The central door is as he remembers it.

I have been here, he tells her.

In your dream.

Yes.

They leave their bicycles in the rack. A small boy in school uniform emerges from the door to the right, bows and greets them, calling Hanako Auntie. He is much younger than the schoolboy in his dream. They bow to him. He invites them in for tea, leads them to the door on the left. West is now filled with fear, can no longer trust himself to know dream from waking. He tells himself that he knows this woman Hanako, that he should not be afraid, that with her it is not important to distinguish dream from waking. It is only an issue with time, isn't it? He has seen certain things in dreams before seeing them awake, that's all. Can happen to anyone.

Still. He breathes his Zen breath, his karate breath, and follows now in the spirit of one going into battle, the spirit of the sparring, the spirit of the sword.

There is an older woman waiting to greet them behind the blue curtains of the left door. She not as old as the woman in his dream and she is not bent but stands from her bow straight and strong and confident, and, like Terayama, looks not at him but into him. She is still beautiful, and perfectly groomed and dressed in a dark kimono and wears a starched, spotless white apron.

Grandmother, Hanako says, this is West-san. Then to him, my grandmother Sakurada.

They bow and say For the first time.

Step up, Mrs. Sakurada says.

They remove their shoes and step up onto polished wood and then through a shoji door onto tatami and kneel at a low table set with tea things. Mrs. Sakurada serves them tea and small cakes, then kneels to face them, slightly back from the table. There is small talk, how well the foreigner uses chopsticks, how pleasant the weather though winter is upon them.

You have come to view the waterfall? she asks.

Yes, Hanako says, if you think it would be all right.

I think so. Though because it is Sunday there may be many people.

That is all right.

More tea?

Hanako finally, almost sadly, West thinks, makes their protracted farewell, promising to stop in again before they return to Imabara. Mrs. Sakurada appears impassive. They go as in his dream around the left side of the building and find the path up to the waterfall. It is wider and longer than in the dream. Two schoolgirls in uniform bow to them as they walk chattering down toward the shop. A few sparrows twitter as they light on low branches. There are no strange animals along the path.

They hear the waterfall before they see it. As they sight the pool he sees that there are stone benches arranged at three points near its edge, two or three people seated silently on each of them. Across the pond, beneath the waterfall, is the bronze figure of a strange, froglike creature, about the size of a middle school child. It grins hungrily at them.

The Kappa, Hanako tells him. Do you know about the Kappa?

No.

He guards the waters and preys on humans. He can be helpful, but he can also be very dangerous.

I see.

Was he in your dream?

Something like him.

Were you afraid of him?

No.

Perhaps you should be, she says.

They walk around the pool, listening to the water falling, enjoying the cool, moist air. The group of hikers in pilgrim garb emerge noisily from path, spread out around the pool and fall silent. The people on the benches rise and leave. West and Hanako follow them at a distance. West is now simply confused by these conflicting realities, time, his perception of time so confused he knows he cannot sort it out, will never be able to. He retreats into Form is Exactly Emptiness, *shiki soku ze ku*, as if it explained something. Tries to remember when it once seemed to, and fails.

Back at the souvenir shop, Hanako leads him in through the central doors, which open on a large room with many traditional Japanese articles displayed for sale. There are inkstones and stationery and brushes, wooden swords and staves, straw hats, dolls in various costumes, ornate scrolls filled with red stamped seals, small carved stones, straw sandals, a variety of vases. Mrs. Sakurada is busy with other customers, two of the people who had preceded them down the path from the waterfall.

West fingers a small, beautifully shaped slate inkstone with a varnished wooden cover.

It is all right for me to buy something? he asks Hanako.

No. She will not let you. If she sees that there is something you want she will make it a gift to you.

Even if I tell her it is a gift for you?

Then she won't let you buy it and will not give it to you.

He quickly retracts his finger from the inkstone, looking away, trying to look at nothing.

They come to a display of sword guards in a glass case. Some are of steel, some of brass. Some of the brass ones are small, not quite round, cut out such that they are mostly air.

Those are for Iaidō swords, she tells him. They are small and narrow so that you don't have to bend your wrist so much, and light for the speed of the draw and the sheathing.

Mrs. Sakurada has finished with her customers, bows them out. Hanako and West approach her as she is returning to her counter.

I would like to buy a sword guard, Hanako tells her

grandmother.

They all go to the display of sword guards, where Hanako points out one of the brass ones for Iaidō. The cut-out metal forms a picture of the Kappa, its mouth shaped in the slot that will fit the sword's blade. Mrs. Sakurada takes it out of the case and beckons Hanako to follow her to the counter, where she wraps it deftly in thin, decorated paper. Then the two women haggle good naturedly over the price. Once settled, no money is offered or requested. The woman hands the package to her granddaughter with both hands and bows, as does Hanako as she takes it with both hands. Hanako then excuses herself and turns to West, offering him the package with both hands, bowing.

To remember this day each time your wield your sword, she says.

Of course he must accept it, though it embarrasses him.

I cannot give you a gift in return? he asks.

Not today, she says.

の

Ever since he has mounted Hanako's gift of the brass guard onto his sword he has known that his cuts are stronger, his draw and sheathing have become smoother and more natural. After his second class using it he places his sword ceremonially in the household shrine, sits staring at the guard, wondering what the Kappa represents to Hanako, what she wants it to mean to him.

He heats a package of ramen, adds half a can of tuna. Heats a small flask of sakê. He eats and drinks at the kitchen table, thumbing through a slim volume listing Japanese family and given names, their characters and meanings. Yamazaki means Mountain Slope. Takeshi means Warrior. Hirano means Wide Plain. Oka, Hill. Ikeda, Pond Field. Terayama means Temple Mountain. Hiroshi means Wide Man. Sakurada means Field of Cherry Blossoms. Hanako means Flower Child.

She is late this Saturday, the last Saturday before New Years. He has bought her an inkstone similar to the one he'd wanted to buy for her at her grandmother's souvenir shop, irregularly shaped. It is flawlessly wrapped in beautiful paper. He places the package next to his book of Japanese names and studies the paper. Its pattern is subtle, has the look of cloth. He remembers how the rough edges of the slate made him think of one of her ikebana vases. He remembers its cover, fitted exactly to the shape of the well, also of slate, the center of it left tall and coarse to serve as a handle. It was surprisingly expensive. He hopes she will like it.

He cleans up after his meal, heats another flask of sakê, takes it and the booklet and the packaged inkstone to the low table in the six-mat room. He sits, sips. He waits for her.

An hour of that and she still has not come. He tidies the table, goes to the kitchen and washes the carafe and the cup, makes up his futon. Changes into his sleeping robe. Lies down and worries, then sleeps.

She comes not long before dawn. Sorry, she says. A Forget the Year party with the ikebana club in Kobê.

I was worried, he admits.

Forgive me.

Yes.

I'll make it up to you.

Yes.

Now.

In the full light of a chilly Sunday morning they start the gas heaters and have tea at the low table. When they have set out the calligraphy things he offers her the package with the inkstone in it. The gift I could not give you in Imabara, he says. She says Thank you, seems reluctant to open it but does finally. She examines the inkstone in much detail, turning it to every angle, her delicate fingers feeling all its surfaces, rough and smooth. She does this with no expression, no word or sound. At last she places it carefully on the felt, kneels most formally and bows deeply to him.

It is beautiful, she says. I will treasure it.

He sighs in relief.

They grind ink and take up brushes. She gives him traditional New Year's samples to copy. As they are cleaning up late in the afternoon, she seems sad. He asks her why.

Because I cannot be with you at the New Year. You know

that I cannot.

Yes, I understand that.

So our wonderful first year ends today.

Yes.

You will write this text on New Year's Day for me?

Yes.

I will write it for you, too. So we will be together in a certain manner.

Yes.

Late, in the futon, she rises and dresses and kneels beside him. Happy New Year, she whispers close to his ear. Her breath shakes him to the very bone.

お

This New Year's Eve he feels he has no choice but to go up the hill to the cemetery to see the bell being rung. Not so cold, this second year, or else he's gotten used to it. Clear and still, and at the shrine just as solemn as the year before. Up there among the gravestones, the enormous bell on its elevated platform under its tiled roof, its half-meter thick, six-meter long log clapper hung from heavy cordage, a line of people on the stairs and into the courtyard below, not even whispering. Two women in brown woolen kimono serving hot, raw sakê, the stuff almost needing to be chewed. He parks his bicycle and watches. The women say Dozo and indicate that he should get into line, they are up to eighty-something in the sequence of a hundred and eight strokes, he'd better hurry.

He gets in line at the foot of the stairs and watches the technique. You go up to the dangling rope attached to the log, fold the hands and bow to the bell. Then you heave back, pulling the log away from the bell, then let its own momentum send it on to strike the great bronze monster. A wonderful sound. Then you bow again and go down the left side of the stairs. No sweat.

He sets his mind free then to consider why they ring it exactly a hundred and eight times. There are a hundred and eight sins. The year, to the Japanese, is quite a discrete identity. Debts must be paid off by the end of it, the slate must be clear and clean at the beginning of the new. The bell's job is to ring out any of the hundred and eight sins the effects of which might linger like bad debts into the new year.

Sins, in Buddhism, aren't like Christian sins. They are those thoughts and actions which impede Enlightenment. Standing now, still on a stairwell, he finds it a comforting notion that the impediments to his Enlightenment are numerable. He hopes that the one he will personally ring out is the right one, the worst.

He goes up to the platform, everyone whispering instructions, the presiding deacon taking him from behind by the shoulders and putting him in position. He bows. He prays during the bow, no words, just an inarticulate cry for purity from somewhere inside.

Whacks the bell with the log in the prescribed manner. Melts with joy at the sheer beauty of the sound, sent out over the city he has come to love, would always love, its people wallowing in their hundred and eight sins just as he does, all struggling for purity just as he does, listen Takamatsu listen Japan listen Asia listen America listen World listen to this bell of wisdom this is the sound this is what you want to hear this is the healing sound the loving sound the living and loving and killing and dying sound this sound this bell this sin cast out by this sound tells us that we are human we are capable of beauty and glory and stupidity and violence for good and evil and if we are not cancer incarnate on the skin of our mother then it is our glory because even if we are cancer it is within the wisdom of nature or it should be he remembers somehow to bow properly after he rings the bell.

And then he goes down and has his cup of raw too-hot sakê and finds his bicycle and rides down the hill and under the JNR and past the Burakumin shanties in icy self-created wind and joins the crowd at Hachiman's shrine and bows to the god. This second year he doesn't draw his fortune at the booth. It isn't fear. He just doesn't need one.

<

Late in May Terayama appears at a sword class. He does not wear his uniform, wields no sword. He is shrunken, darkened, only his eyes seeming alive. He speaks quietly with Nomura-sensei, then sits to watch the formal class.

For the last several months West has not been singled out for Nomura's criticism, but neither has he been particularly praised. He holds his position at the back of the class, concentrates intensely, occasionally disappears. He is sure that Nomura sees this and that Terayama will too.

When the First Level exercises are over West is told to withdraw, to sit near the door and watch. The rest of the class performs the intermediate set, after which Hirano withdraws to sit beside him. They watch the older men perform the advanced set. At the end of that session the seniors bow out and go to the tatami room to change. West is brought front and center and told to perform the First Level set without instruction or pause.

He remembers it all. No redoubling, no effort. For most of this performance he disappears, hears the whispers of his uniform on the polished wooden floor, hears the whistle of his cuts, feels the cool of his oiled blade as it flashes from the sheath and slides silently back into it. When he is finished he bows to the spirit in the sword and truly feels it and thinks he may now understand Sword Cuts Illusory Lightning.

Neither Terayama nor Nomura comment, just signal him to withdraw and sit. Hirano then is told to perform the intermediate set. So far as West can see he does it perfectly. When he is finished he comes to sit next to West while the two teachers confer in whispers.

Hirano-san, Nomura says, do you have a Senkyo Sect name?

Yes, Sensei. It is Kyoshin.

Good. You will be given the Intermediate Certificate.

Thank you, Sensei.

West-san, you will be given a Senkyo Sect name and the First Level certificate.

Thank you, Sensei.

Dismissed.

All bow. Nomura-sensei withdraws to change in the teachers' room, West and Hirano to the room for students. Terayama remains sitting, staring at something only he can see.

As they are folding their uniforms, Hirano says to West, We should celebrate. This is an honor for both of us.

Yes.

We'll go to dinner and drink sakê.

Yes.

The hall is empty and darkened. They bow to the front and slide the door closed. It is very dark in the alleyway behind the building where they have left their bicycles. They fumble with them. Hirano is faster, has wheeled his bike out to where there is a dim streetlight. From next to the rack a shadow moves, speaks.

West-san. It is the thin, attenuated voice of Terayama.

Yes, Sensei.

I will come to you next Saturday morning. Dress for the street early.

Yes, Sensei.

The shadow disappears.

They cycle to Hirano's favorite restaurant, order sakê, pour for one another. Kampai. Banzai. Congratulations.

Yes, but for what exactly?

You have been certified as competent in the Shoden, the first set of sword exercises. And you have been accepted as a sort of monk in the Senkyo Sect, symbolized by your receiving a Buddhist name.

I see. Your name, Kyoshin, wasn't it? What does it mean?

It means Entrusted with the Doctrine, more or less. I guess it might also mean Trust in the Doctrine.

How do they choose the names?

They take one character from Senkyo, either Sen, Wellspring, or Kyo, Doctrine. Then they add a second one based on something they know about you. Your strongest characteristic.

I see. Do you know Terayama-sensei's name?

Yes. It is Reikyo. Maybe Doctrine of the Spirit. Or Spirit of the Doctrine.

Thank you. It's good to know. Do you know what mine will be?

No. They will give you a certificate that tells it.

She is not there when he gets home. Perhaps she came and left because he was so late? He showers, makes up the futon. He lies aponder. He has a new name and he doesn't know what it is. He has a Special Assignment which will be performed in that new name. He doesn't know who it is that will kill Bankyo, but knows whoever it is will not be named West.

He dreams again of the pool and the waterfall. Near the end of the dream he feels her near him warm and soft, she touches him never looking at the Kappa and he gradually awakens to darkness and her warmth and says Hanako. She says nothing but strokes him and soon he is new again.

The following Saturday morning Terayama arrives. He carries a small suitcase and is dressed in a pinstripe and tie. The suit looks as if it were made for a much larger man. West greets him, still in his sleeping robe, shocked by the old man's withered appearance.

Terayama slips off his shoes, sits on the edge of the wooden floor and opens his case. From it he withdraws a large envelope. West sees him into the six-mat room, then goes to the kitchen to boil water. They then sit at the low table. Terayama sips his foul-smelling tea, then clears a space and opens the envelope.

This is your First Level certificate, he says. Can you read it?

He turns it upright and places it before West.

Yes, Sensei. It says that I have been certified in official testing to have completed the Shoden requirements in Iaidō. It is signed and sealed by you, as Reikyo.

That is correct. Now, this one is your Buddhist name. Can you read it? He slides this one over on top of the Shoden certificate.

This one is more difficult. He can make out some of it, but he will need his dictionaries for the rest.

I can see again that you signed and sealed it, but no, Sensei. I cannot read it without my dictionary.

You can do that later. It gives you a priest's name. It is Kansen.

Kansen. Contemplate the Wellspring.

Thank you, Sensei. I am very grateful.

He is in fact overwhelmed. To be given a name one has earned!

They get into a taxi waiting in front of the shrine. Terayama gives an address in the Hyogo-machi, near the station. On the way, West tries to look at Takamatsu with Kansen's eyes. It is all familiar now, home to him, but still fascinating, foreign, and beautiful. West's eyes, or Kansen's? He has no idea.

They get out in front of a shop he has seen many times but has never particularly noticed. It is that of a seal carver, a man who makes out of stone and wood and horn the ubiquitous red signatures seen on documents and scrolls everywhere. Miss Oka, at Yamazaki Industries, keeps one with his name on it, a small oval one, uses it to deposit his monthly salary into his bank account for him. He knows nothing more about them.

The seal maker is an old, scrawny fellow wearing thick eyeglasses. He bows deeply to Terayama, addressing him as Hoshi. This is very formal, and means, roughly, exalted priest. Terayama calls the sealmaker Nishidera-san, introduces West first as West-san, then as Kansen-gobosan, the somewhat less exalted priest. Deep bows again. Terayama asks for paper and brush. The old man places a folded sheet on the counter, inks and points up a small brush. Terayama writes the two characters for Kansen, the three for the Senkyo Sect, then writes the two characters meaning No Mind. There then ensues a long and detailed conversation between Terayama and Nishidera, filled with terms and references West can only guess at. When there is a pause as Nishidera goes to his supply of stones, Terayama asks West the date of his birth.

Ah, Year of the Dragon, Terayama says when West has

told him. Good. He then repeats this to Nishidera, who nods, his back to them as he pores over his collection.

You will need eight seals, Terayama tells him. Two big ones, about two and a half centimeters. One will have white characters on a red background and will read Senkyo-ryu No. It will go above when you write scroll-sized pieces. The other will be red characters on a white background and will read just Kansen. It goes below. Then you will have two that read Mushin, No Mind. They will be the same height as the other two, but will be half as wide. One will have red letters and one white. Do you understand?

Understood.

The other four will be much smaller, about one centimeter high. Those will be for small writing, like haiku.

Then there is much discussion as Terayama and Nishidera leaf through style books and a copy of the *I Ching*, Nishidera drawing with the small brush different ways to place the characters in the squares. Eventually they come to an agreement, at which point they begin examining the collection of stones Nishidera has brought to the counter. Several of them have intricately sculpted dragons on the top.

In the end they choose one large square and one small one with dragon tops, all the rest plain. The colors of the stones range from an almost-white gray to a deep reddish brown. Nishidera tells them that they will be finished one week from today, then figures the prices on an abacus, writes a figure in Chinese characters.

You must let me pay him, West-san, Terayama says. Then they will be gifts from me, and will have much more power and value. It will give the work more meaning to Nishidera-san, and more meaning over the years to you.

Thank you, Sensei.

Again he is overwhelmed, this time with an edge of fear

added. When and how will these bills come due?

Terayama is clearly tired, but insists he can walk the short distance to the station to board his train to Zentsuji. West walks with him, sees him to the platform.

Don't be late to sword class, Terayama says.

I will be on time, Sensei. And I thank you so very much again.

They exchange bows, West's deep, long, and filled with sincerity. Terayama boards, takes a seat by the window where West can see him. As the train jolts into motion, the old man smiles at him and raises his hand in what appears to be a benediction.

ま

The next Saturday he cycles to the sealmaker's shop on the way to sword class. The old, bent man welcomes him in, even though he is in the process of shutting down for the day. As for tea, time for this, is there? he asks West.

Yes, time there is, thank you.

Seeing the sword case and sports bag, he asks, As for sword class, what time?

Six, not until.

Good. As for the seals, I will show you how to use them.

They sit on the tatami at his low table. The sealmaker brews and serves tea, then takes a seal and a small, round, porcelain jar, some paper. He opens the jar to reveal a bed of red goo.

Seal meat this is called, he says. He dabs the stone seal lightly and repeatedly on the surface of the red stuff, occasionally examining the surface of the stone, until he is satisfied with its quantity. Then he presses the reddened surface of the stone to a piece of paper. Exactly parallel to the edge, he says. Then he takes a small brush and writes what is perhaps a signature on the vertical, reddens the seal again, presses it just below the last character. Lined up and centered exactly, he says.

Thank you, sensei.

Sensei not, he says. Nishidera only.

The package the old man gives him is larger than he expected, and somewhat heavier. He bows his thanks, packs it into his sports bag between the pieces of his uniform. They bow to one another several times, say Sayonara, and West pushes off on his bicycle, feeling grateful yet again, both to Terayama-sensei and Nishidera-san.

Her spike-heeled shoes are neatly paired in the vestibule when he gets home from class. She is in the six-mat room at the table, wearing her sleeping robe and writing what appear to be signatures with the small brush.

You will want to write your new name somewhat like this, perhaps, she tells him. Here, she says rising, I will make you a drink, and you can practice it a few times while I prepare dinner.

He sits, seeing Kansen written several times, in different styles, ranging from block to extremely cursive. He takes a fresh sheet and begins to copy them, the block style first. She brings him a whiskey, looks over his shoulder. The block style looks good, she says. You have practiced that before.

All week long, he admits.

Then try the semi-cursive for a while.

He does.

Dinner is almost ready, she says from the kitchen. Please clean the table now.

He does. Dinner is of lightly sautéed shrimp and white rice, Takuan pickles, a seaweed salad, heated saké.

You have your seals now? she asks.

Yes. I have not yet opened the package.

We will look at them together tomorrow. Did Nishidera-san teach you how to use them?

Yes. A brief lesson with a small signature seal.

I will teach you the rest tomorrow.

Thank you.

After dinner she clears and cleans while he showers, changes into a sleeping robe, makes up the futon.

Kansen, she whispers in his ear as she lies beside him. It is the first time she has called him by his new name and it sends a shiver all through him.

Later he asks her, Do you also have a Buddhist name?

Yes, four of them.

Four?

Yes. One for tea, one for flowers, one for calligraphy, and one for everything else.

Can you tell me that one?

It is Eisen. It means Gifted Wellspring.

They always get it right, don't they.

Perhaps not always.

This time, certainly.

You are kind to say so.

They stop talking and much later they drift into sleep.

The morning arrives bright and gilding and clean-smelling. They share a shower, something new, exciting. Their shower takes a long time and all the hot water.

After a light breakfast he sets up the table for calligraphy. He goes to his sports bag, takes out the package of seals. He sits with her at the table and unwraps it. The seals are in a beautifully lacquered box. He opens it reverently. Inside, the box is divided into compartments. One has a silk-covered box containing the seal meat in a porcelain jar, just like Nishidera-san's. One contains the set of four small seals, another the set of the larger ones. She chooses some practice sheets he has written earlier, tells him to sign them. Then she shows him where the seals—three to each sheet—are meant to go. She teaches him to redden the stones correctly. It takes him several tries to get that right, and many more to place the seals correctly.

Correctly, she says, is never the same for any two pieces.

Just as with the black, the red must balance with the white. Many pieces are ruined by misplacement of the seals. Learning how to do this beautifully takes a long time.

She brings in her big satchel, takes out a cardboard tube. In it is the piece she had asked for from him, the one she said he'd written so well, Sword Cuts Illusory Lightning.

She wets his small brush and shows him where to sign his new name on the side of the sheet. He writes it on practice paper a few times to get the scale and the style and then writes it on the finished piece where she tells him to place it. She places the seals for him, two beneath the signature, the half-width Mushin one in the upper right corner. Then with a push pin hangs it in his household shrine, sits formally and watches it.

I will have it mounted in silk for a hanging scroll, she says. Thank you again for giving it to me.

It is nothing.

Now show me all the others you have written on good paper.

He goes to the closet and brings out a fat roll of them. Together they unroll the long, narrow strips, laying them out on the mats. They sort them into the dozen or so traditional texts, re-roll all but one of these stacks. She then stands back and has him lay the first and second in the pile side by side.

The second one is better. Put the other aside.

He does so. She looks now at the new pair. Two is still better. Put Three aside with One.

And so on until she has chosen the one best. This one he puts on the table. He rolls up the others and them puts aside. They continue the process through all of the different texts until there are ten sheets rolled up on the table. He combines all the others into a single roll and returns them to the closet.

These you must burn someday, when you can have a fire. When you burn them, set your mind on writing better next time.

Yes.

They sit to the table then and he signs and places the seals on all of the ones she has chosen, under her direction. He ruins the first one by smearing a seal, and another by writing his signature awkwardly. In the end he has eight he can keep. Eight out of nearly a hundred.

These too you can have mounted in silks. Kagawa-hyogusan in the Ta-machi does beautiful work.

Thank you. I will.

They eat vinegar rice and seaweed for lunch and settle into the futon for the afternoon. All the sounds of traffic from the street and chatter from the shrine fade away as she whispers. Kansen, she whispers, Kansen. Eisen, he whispers, Eisen. She teaches him new things to do for her, and she does new things for him. Mysterious things. Even frightening things. She turns herself into a fox, turns him into the Kappa. As the afternoon slips into evening he sleeps and dreams of the fox and the Kappa and when he wakes in the gray before dawn she is gone. She has remembered to take the scroll out of the alcove, and has left him a poem in return, not a haiku but in haiku form:

All things are passing
In this world of constant change;
All but consciousness.

け

He is aware of a new fierceness in himself, now that he is Kansen, Contemplate the Wellspring, he must guard this Wellspring he now contemplates and avenge its betrayal by Bankyo, who once was entrusted with its defense and almost destroyed it. He becomes the Kappa at the same time, hungry for human flesh, filled with magic powers. His speed and strength have no limits in this evening's karate class. His mind is empty, this awareness of himself is not mental, it comes from his center, burns in his center, spreads steam from his center to all of the rest of him, he is lathered with sweat, his karate uniform soaked from the time the class has finished the opening stretches, blocks, punches, kicks and formal kata exercises. When they line up to face each other for sparring he is calm and wild at once, his breathing is gentle perhaps but that is all that is gentle in him, he hungers and rages in the center of total calm, the center of a hurricane, Kansen has become the guardian before the temple, the Kappa drools in hunger, he faces his first opponent and before the call Begin! has ceased to echo in the hall he has struck with a shout and won.

Facing his second opponent he is no longer hungry no longer fierce he is ready to wait and watch like the Kappa like the cat his opponent is a mouse he waits and enjoys the waiting somewhere in his body then the instant comes, the mouse has a hint of fear in its eyes he pounces and wins again.

He doesn't know how many opponents he has beaten when the call Stop! comes. He does not relax, does not have to relax he is already relaxed. Arakawa-sensei faces him at sparring distance. Now me, he says. They bow. The head student calls Begin!

The sensei gives him no opening. He waits. Then the sensei slackens faintly, he sees the drop of a shoulder perhaps and he pounces and his strike is blocked and he is hit, hit well, in the center. They back off and bow to one another.

Now you, Arakawa says to the head student, a fourth-degree black belt.

The head student is a harsh tank of a man, as tall as Kansen, but twice as wide. They bow to one another and the sensei calls Begin! The head student strikes immediately but it is a feint Kansen blocks the feint and is struck well in the center. They back off and bow.

Now you, the sensei says to Hirano.

Kansen does not know it is Hirano, he sees only the opponent the sensei calls Begin! he shifts his stance slightly the opponent does not try to strike when he does but waits as Kansen waits time stops then Kansen drops a shoulder slightly just as the sensei had done and the opponent mis-reads it as a slackening and strikes as Kansen had done with the sensei and Kansen blocks the strike and strikes to the head and he has won again. They step back and bow to one another.

Line up! the sensei calls. They fall into line. The sensei whispers to the head student, who leaves at a trot. The sensei sits formally and the class follows and all sit formally. Silently.

The head student trots back into the hall. He is carrying something black in his left hand. He stands next to Arakawa-sensei, who stands and calls Kansen by the name Kansen. Kansen rises and runs to face the sensei. The head student walks around him to stand at his back. The sensei unties the knot of Kansen's brown belt and strips it away. The head student behind him arcs a black belt over his head and pulls it tight around his center, then crosses it in back and hands the dangling ends forward. The sensei takes the ends and ties the knot in front.

Congratulations! he shouts.

The class shouts Congratulations!

All bow, and class is dismissed.

We must celebrate, Hirano says as they are dressing. You will come to dinner?

Yes.

They go to their usual restaurant and order saké, look over the selection of dishes. When the saké comes they pour for one another, say Kampai, drink, then pour again.

This was very unusual, Hirano says. To give a black belt without formal testing. But then, your karate tonight was very unusual too.

I was Kansen, West says. And I was the Kappa. I was not present.

It was somewhat like that for me, too. I was Kyoshin, but I was never the Kappa or any other mythic animal. I was never that good, either.

They order their food. While they wait for it to be grilled they drink more saké and order two more bottles.

Were you one of my opponents? West asks.

Yes, the last one.

Why did they want me to fight you?

To see if you could win again after losing to Arakawa-sensei and the head student, and if you could beat a second-degree black belt. And to see if facing your friend would make a difference.

I see.

Their order arrives, seared scallops and skewered shrimp and seaweed salad and two small bowls of rice. They pour saké and take up chopsticks and eat with the relish of hunger and wonderful food.

As they walk back toward their bicycles along the Marugame-machi Hirano says, You made not one slip. When your shoulder dropped, I thought it meant that you had slipped because you were tired. I was wrong. You blocked my strike and hit me in the same instant.

I think I had just learned to drop the shoulder when Sensei beat me. That's how I did it with you?

Yes.

I didn't know.

The only way it ever works is when you don't know.

They reach Yamazaki Industries, find their bicycles under the stairway, wheel them out onto the covered street. To his own surprise, West says, Thank you for all you have done for me.

I have done little, Hirano says.

You have done much. So have Yamazaki Industries and Terayama-sensei and all of the Senkyo Sect. I thank you.

It has been nothing, Hirano says, but his eyes drift as he says it.

When he reaches his apartment he showers and bathes and lays out the futon and tries to assess what has happened and cannot, cannot even remember what has happened. He drifts with a mind both cluttered and empty. Feels a bruise developing near the base of his sternum where either Arakawa-sensei or the head student hit him and so remembers being hit but nothing else.

Soon he sleeps, a blank and empty sleep, but a movement in the night wakes him to the pain of the bruise on his sternum. He shifts to a position where it doesn't hurt and stares at the shoji screen covering his window overlooking the shrine. It glows from the outside with the yellow residue of the streetlight below. He is aware of a confusion of leftover dream images, of a Noh dancer he knows is Hanako despite her mask, of the Kappa grinning malevolently, of a fox watching him from the shadows in a dense forest. The souvenir shop. The pond. He drifts slowly back toward sleep.

He enters a cave, the entrance is a crevasse between two huge boulders that lean against each other, forming an arch. It is dim in the cave but not dark. He sees a form, it is the monk he had dreamed of who sat under the waterfall covered by an ornate robe. He goes closer to the figure and sees that what in the earlier dream seemed to be a grin is now the monk's torn cheek, exposing his teeth. The monk is dead, long dead, the body desiccated, the skin dark parchment. It is a mummy.

He looks down the long and narrow cave and sees another, its face not torn but the fingers of its right hand missing, lying in a heap in its lap. And another. And another. A long row of them, all under ornate robes, stretching back into the cave as far as the light reaches. He knows they are the mummies of the Senkyo temple. Terayama stands at his side and says Soon I will be one of them.

He wakes again out of this dream and looks at the shoji. The light behind it is no longer the yellow of the streetlight but the gray of early dawn.

Usually he would have been up and on his way to the Zen temple for meditation by now, but it is already too late, it is the first time he has missed it. He realizes how much the sparring has taken out of him. Yet despite the dreams he has slept well, feels refreshed, fit but for the bruised sternum. He showers and performs some karate stretches and then sits before his household shrine. He chants the Heart Sutra and then closes his eyes and meditates. He doesn't know for how long. When he returns to his place on the tatami in front of his shrine he chants the Four Vows. Then goes to his kitchen and makes coffee.

He is sitting at the table and sipping his coffee when there is a knock on his door and a mumbled greeting. He slips into his wooden sandals at the vestibule and opens the door to Terayama-sensei. The old man is dressed in casual clothes, a ball cap, a windbreaker, laced boots. His clothes are wet.

Dress like this, Terayama says We are going on a trip. We will do some hiking. Pack for a few days, just essentials. Karate clothes. You will not need your sword. Oh, and your dictionary.

Yes, Sensei. But, Yamazaki Industries. . . .

They know. It's all right.

Yes, Sensei.

Hurry please. A cab waits.

Yes, Sensei.

He doesn't have a ball cap, stuffs a beret in the pocket of his raincoat. He doesn't have hiking boots either, but has a pair of split-toes cloth boots like the laborers wear, hopes that they will do. Sports bag, two karate suits, one white and one black. Underwear, split-toed socks. His shaving kit, a pair of jeans and a sweatshirt. As he is putting on the cloth boots in the vestibule, Terayama tells him to bring the wooden sandals. Then they are off to the station in the cab through the rain.

They can't get a direct train, have to change in Tadotsu. Their train is not an express but not a milk train either, four stops before Tadotsu. It is waiting for them, not very full. Terayama is asleep before it leaves. West returns to his hobby of listening to passing conversations in Japanese. He thinks he might be getting the hang of it.

He watches the country going by in the thin rain. They slow for but don't stop at stations in small villages or suburbs; he sometimes can read the names but doesn't know how to pronounce them. One intrigues him: the character for devil followed by *mu*. The meaning is clear: Without devils. A good place to live. They stop in Sakaide, Leaving the Slopes, and in Marugame, Round (or perhaps, fat) Turtle. No more than three or four minutes each. In Marugame is a long wooden building through the dirty windows of which he sees a rack of bamboo and wooden swords on the wall, a kendo school.

In Tadotsu, Every Time Port, Terayama wakes up and stands, almost in the same impulse. Change here, he mutters, and they get off the train.

They go for tea and hot water at a kiosk outside the station building, stand sipping it from styrofoam cups. The rain is lighter here, but the gutters on the roof over the platform pour a gurgling stream into a ditch next to the tracks. Fog shrouds the hills to the west.

The train to Kotohira arrives. They board it with a few other passengers. As they move southward he looks out the window, follows the gray-green of the rain on the hills past the railroad shacks and the thick web of power lines. The train stops at Zentsuji, Goodness Trafficking Temple. In the distance he catches glimpses of old, old temples.

We will come back here later, Terayama says. You will enjoy the temple of Kukai.

At Kotohira, Peace of the Koto, as West reads the characters on the station signboard, they walk through the little town—consisting mainly of curio shops and little restaurants—and start the long climb up to the shrine buildings. They don't go all the way up to the main hall, but pay their respects from a landing where the endless stairs turn, only the roof of the main hall in sight. Then they turn back, go down a short distance, and make a detour into a large white, tile-roofed building, quite different in design from the others. It proves to be an art museum.

We are here only to see one thing, Terayama says, leading the way through the exhibits.

They pass many interesting objects, sculptures, swords, suits of armor. At last they stop before a hanging scroll, battered, torn and water-stained. The painting is in black ink thinned to several shades of gray, a landscape of a bleak valley with crows flying over. With a start, West recognizes the faint red seal. It reads Niten, Two Heavens.

Musashi, he says, startled.

Miyamoto Musashi, perhaps the most famous samurai of all, author of *The Book of Five Rings*.

Yes. Terayama grins. Wasn't it worth the climb?

They race to the station and board a train back to Zentsuji. The train starts moving before they can even find seats. The car is empty and smells damp and is chilly. They take seats near the back, close to the door. West shoves their luggage onto the rack above, then slips past Terayama, who has left him the window seat. The window is streaked with rain, obscuring the beauty of the richly soaked hills.

We will go to the Zentsuji temple to pay our respects to the memory of Kukai, Terayama says, once they're in their seats. He was born there.

West knows that Kukai had been the founder of the Shingon sect in Japan, but has always associated him with Koya-san, far to the northeast. He had no idea he'd been born in Zentsuji. The only other thing he knows about him is that legend has it that he had invented the Japanese phonetic system, hiragana, and that the legend is disputed.

Is it true that Kukai invented hiragana? he asks.

Perhaps not, Terayama answers. But he did compose the i-ro-ha poem. Do you know it?

Yes. It uses all the forty-eight syllables to tell a summary of Buddhist thought. It's still used in that order sometimes, the way we use the alphabet to list things, items A, B, C and so on. I have it memorized.

Can you translate it into English?

It has been done, though I may have done it a little differently. He closes his eyes and visualizes the characters.

Colors and fragrances soon fade.
In our world, nothing lasts forever.
So today, cross over the deep mountains of existing things,
And there will be no more idle dreams,
No more intoxication.

Terayama stares out the window for a time, then says, Sounds pretty good. Not much rhythm in English, though. The old man closes his eyes. It is a short trip. Again he wakes just as the train begins to slow.

They walk through the rain to the Zentsuji temple. This is the very oldest Shingon temple in all of Japan, Terayama tells him as they near the gate. Re-built many times, of course. It is on land donated by Kukai's father. There is a picture of Kukai in that hall over there.

They go to look at the picture, but the building is closed for repairs. Terayama bows deeply, sits formally, and stays there, chanting. West joins him, listening to the chant but not understanding it. When Terayama finishes they rise and walk toward the main hall.

It is said that Kukai is the first Japanese to reach Nirvana in his own living body, Terayama whispers. I was asking him to help me with his example, so I can do it, too.

Where is his body now? West asks.

It is a secret. No one knows, although almost certainly it is somewhere on Koya-san.

The main hall is open, quite large, with a large Buddha. When West asks, he is surprised to learn that it is the Yakushi Buddha, rather than the Dainichi. After Terayama bows and sits and chants again, he explains a little more.

I prayed to Yakushi because he is the Buddha of healing, especially of medicines, as I suppose you know. But while the mind is the most important thing in reaching Nirvana, the plants and herbs I eat, and have been eating, are very important too. So I prayed to Yakushi that my diet is right.

They stand, bounce on their toes to restore circulation to numbed legs. The rain has eased into what is little more than a mist. Now we will find a taxi and go to the dojo, the old man says.

It is late afternoon. A slanting shaft of golden sunlight

strikes their faces. Terayama grabs West by the arm and turns him around to the east. There is a rainbow arching over the temple behind them.

West smiles as Terayama breaks into joyous laughter.

The dojo is on the upper floor of a row of shops facing a covered street, a miniature version of the Marugame-machi in Takamatsu. All the shops below deal in traditional wares, medicinal herbs, an acupuncture and shiatsu clinic, a vegetarian restaurant that serves only monk's fare. It is twilight, the shops are closing, the streetlights blink on one by one. Terayama leads him up the narrow stairway to a wide vestibule and a sliding door. They remove their shoes. Terayama slides the door open, they bow to the vast, empty room, wood-floored, but with the inner half covered with mats. A small wooden shrine hangs high on a wall, and all round the room at eye level are pine panels covered with calligraphy. West recognizes the characters naming all of the sword exercises.

Come, Terayama says, and leads him across the hall.

At the far end is a smaller sliding door. The old man opens it, waves West in. It is a four-and a half-mat room with a low table, a small shoji-screened window, a closet behind another sliding door. In the closet is a folded futon, and on a shelf a writing box and a stack of papers for writing the Heart Sutra.

This will be your room while you are here, Terayama tells him. You will copy the sutra every day.

Yes, Sensei.

Then he shows him to an adjacent room, a large, modern bathroom with three shower stalls and a washing machine and a dryer. On one wall a row of brown monk's robes hang on pegs. Terayama points to the last one on the left.

This one is yours, he says. You will wear it first thing in the morning, for meditation, and then when you copy the sutra.

Yes, Sensei.

They return to the small tatami room.

Be awake and ready before dawn. And remember, only the sensei speaks. The students may answer him only to say yes or no or I don't understand.

Yes, Sensei.

While you are here, you will be called Kansen-gobosan. You will not be West anymore.

Yes, Sensei.

Sayonara, he says, bowing. West bows and says Sayonara and Terayama withdraws, closing the sliding door. His footsteps are almost silent, though a plank squeaks once. West hears the outer door slide open and shut. It occurs to him that it is the first day of June. He wonders how long he will be in this strange place.

He slides open the shoji screen covering his window. The glass can be opened, but outside it is barred. The view is not of a covered street but of tiled roofs curved like swords, a row of plum trees still losing their blooms, and evergreen mountains beyond, gleaming in the last rays of sun.

こ

He wakes with a start in darkness. There is the least glow through the shoji-screened window, but it is yellowish, not gray. He has seen no clock, has no watch. He assesses his condition, decides that he has slept long and well enough. He looks out through the window. It is still night. How is he to know if it's nearly dawn?

He hears footsteps on the stairs, and knows he must have been awakened by the sound of the door below. Hurriedly he rises, goes to the bathroom, runs cold water on his face, dons his new monk's robe. The lights in the main hall blink on just as he emerges from the bathroom. He sees an older man in slacks and a white shirt, bows to him. The man returns a perfunctory bow, goes to a small door on the opposite side of the four- and a half-mat room, emerges with a cushion and a pair of wood blocks. He places these at the edge of matted section of the floor. West hasn't moved. The man walks to him, then around behind him, grasps him by the shoulders and guides him onto the wood, to a corner opposite the main doorway. Then he goes into the bathroom, and in a few minutes comes out dressed in his monk's robe. He kneels into formal position on the wood, to the right of where he's placed the cushion and wood blocks. West folds himself into the same position.

They arrive in twos and threes, perhaps twenty of them, dressed in sports clothes or civilian casual. All go to the bathroom, reappear in their robes, then sit formally in various places on the wooden floor. No smiles or bows to one another, no eye contact.

Terayama arrives, bows to the room. He is already in his robes. He walks silently to the cushion, sits in Lotus position. Intones, *Hannya haramita shin gyō*.

This is the strongest chanting of the sutra West has yet experienced. These men are not office girls or students or clerks. He is not ready to say what they are, but the power of their voices makes him shiver. He hears his own chanting with them, and feels a part of something massive, transcendent. When the sutra ends the silence is even more massive.

Their meditation is longer than it had been in Takamatsu, though he is made aware of that only when the shocking clap of the wood blocks arrives. These men do not uncoil themselves, stretch legs, all that. They stand straight up on their dead legs and bounce. West does the same, and the agony is exquisite.

All pause for a moment, standing perfectly still. They bow to Terayama, who remains in the Lotus position and bows from it. Then they fold hands in front of their sashes and walk in step, forming a line that row by row traces the shape of the room. As each man passes the rack of wooden swords he takes one. West is of course last. He does the same.

They form two lines, ten men in each. The men in one of the lines place their backs to one of the long walls. Those in the second line to the other wall, so they face each other in pairs. West is the eleventh man in the second line.

What follows is a set of memorized sword exercises in pairs, clearly well-known to all but him. He follows along as best he can, trying to copy the movements of the man next to him. This is nothing like the sword training he knew in Takamatsu. He is fuddled, but has no idea what else to do. The noise of colliding wood swords is loud and often accompanied by shouts which distract him.

This phase of the class ends abruptly. He notices that Terayama has moved, stands quietly on a far corner of the mat. One pair of swordsmen move up to the matted area. The others line up to sit and watch. All but one, who instead walks to West and bows. West bows too. The man is in early middle-age, smiles pleasantly.

For the next hour and more West receives private instruction in the first two sets of wood sword pairs, trying not to be distracted by the occasional shouts and clashes from the activity on the mats. The instruction is in great detail and slow motion at first, but as he comes to adopt the postures and perform the movements to his instructor's satisfaction, the speed increases and West finds he is having great fun, and is disappointed when Terayama calls Stop.

All line up again and go through formal bows with the wood swords, the same as those with the real ones used in Takamatsu. Terayama has resumed the Lotus position in his place on the mats. They meditate again. After the clap of the blocks they chant the Four Vows sutra, then rise with their swords and walk in line to rack them. As the others go to change clothes, Terayama signals him to approach.

Change into karate uniform, he says. White. Wait in the small room.

He does as he is told, waits listening as the others change and pack and leave with muttered Sayonaras. When the last has gone Terayama calls his name. Karate time, he says.

West steps out onto the mats and bows. Terayama is off on the wood floor, signals him over.

This karate is different, he says. Look at the floor.

West sees that where Terayama is standing the floor has a circle some eight feet across etched into it, divided by eight etched diameters. He has not noticed this before.

Stand on the circle, across from me.

Yes, Sensei.

Terayama takes an odd, bird-like posture. Stand like this, he says.

West copies the stance as best he can.

Don't move. Don't speak.

Terayama scurries to him, corrects his posture by nudging a foot and shifting an arm, then scurries back to the other side of the circle.

Good. Now move like me.

And so they begin to move around the circle very slowly, like wading birds.

Stay exactly opposite me, Terayama tells him. Exactly.

They go around several times, then change postures and go around the other way several more. At a certain point Terayama says Stop, and leads him off the wood onto the mats. There they resume the circling, but without the inscribed circle on the wood.

You must do this with no-mind. There is just the circle and the opponent. Soon there will also be no-circle and no-opponent.

Yes, Sensei.

They continue with this for a long time. Suddenly West breaks out in a sweat, soaking his karate uniform. Though his concentration has been good, he is instantly aware that something has gone wrong. He clings to no-mind, but becomes aware of the clinging. Immediately he stumbles from the heavy blow to his solar plexus, saves his air, but plunges down flat on his backside, shaking his head. Terayama-sensei is standing eight feet away, hands folded over the sash securing his brown monk's robe, and it's clear that he has never struck.

I don't understand, West says.

Stand up, Terayama says.

West stands quickly, assumes his master's posture and bows. Terayama bows too.

This is the first time you have seen this, Terayama says.

This is what you are here to learn. We call it Already Hit. So you don't have to hit anyone, you just make him think he's been hit. That's what happened.

Terayama takes a new stance, West matches it. They begin again to move in the Circle of Eight. After about two minutes of this West feels himself charge at Terayama, landing a solid punch. Then suddenly from nowhere he feels the tap on his throat. Terayama is close in his face.

I don't understand, he says.

That was another one. We call it Threw the Punch. In that one, you make your opponent think he has already hit you, so you can then hit him unawares. These take a long time to learn, as do the defenses against them. Mostly it depends on the depth of your meditation.

Yes, Sensei.

You learn them by doing your exercises. By knowing the stances completely and naturally. By meditating in total emptiness. Meditate for long times in the stances, not just sitting.

Yes, Sensei, West says, but doesn't quite believe this.

Practice this all day until your meal. Someone will bring that to you at noon and leave a tray at the sliding door. You are not to open the door until that person has left. Then when you are finished, leave the tray outside where you found it. Do not try to see the person who will collect it. After that, write the sutra and rest. Karate class will begin at six. Some students will arrive before that. Karate will hurt. You will suffer Already Hit and Threw the Punch many times. It is the only way to learn how to defend against it.

Yes, Sensei.

With this Terayama bows and leaves. West bows to his back, watches him slide the door open and then closed, hears his wooden sandals on the stairs and hears the outer door open and close and hears what he is sure is the setting of the lock. Some time later he goes down the stairs and checks. The door is locked. He is a prisoner.

え

Months have passed. The daily schedule never varies. Following morning meditation led by Terayama, classes are held in the vast, high-ceilinged, wood-floored hall, sword before dawn, more meditation and karate in the evening. After the sword class, Terayama gives him two hours of private instruction in karate. His daily meal—brown rice, pickles, seaweed, some vegetables, buckwheat tea—is brought up to him from the restaurant below at noon on a tray which is left outside the sliding door with a quiet knock and an apologetic phrase. In the afternoons he copies the Heart Sutra. Karate is now entirely about Already Hit and Threw the Punch. He and all the younger students simply get battered, over and over; there seems no end to it. Some part of him always hurts from the countless falls and blows. Terayama assures him often that he is improving, but nothing hurts any less than it did the first time.

After the meal is the hardest time. After eating he looks out his window, now at the snow-covered tiles and bared plum branches of February, remembers that it was the first day of June when he had packed only for a few days. In all this time he has not left the dojo once. This is the time when he feels incarcerated and wonders how long it will go on. He has never been told. All he knows is that it is all right with Yamazaki Industries, and that his Takamatsu apartment is secure. He lies down on the tatami mats in the small room and loses control of his mind. Hanako. The noon bell. The view of the cemetery, the view of the shrine.

Hanako. He has not heard from her, no longer can even hope for her poems in the mail. The sight of her, the feel of her, the smell of her subtle perfumes. This is the time he thinks of bolting, returning to Takamatsu, finding her, having her, keeping her.

Yet he knows he will not, cannot. He knows that if he did that she would not have him, that he must see this all the way through to whatever end it leads. He knows this, but after the meal there is no comfort in the knowing.

Still, he can do this. He must do this. For his Special Assignment.

He gets up and looks out his window again. This he admits, is a good view too though today he cannot see the mountains for the mist. It even has bells, several of them, though all more distant and none so booming as the cemetery's.

He dons his priest's robe, uses the toilet, and with a sigh sits to the low table and grinds ink. By the time the ink is thick enough his mind is clear, the columns of characters in the sutra calm him, let him focus. For the next few hours he disappears into them. Late in the afternoon the early karate students begin to arrive, change into their uniforms, practice singly or in pairs in the big hall. West cleans his brush and inkstone in the bathroom sink, changes into his karate uniform and joins them.

The six or eight students are a mix of high school students and old men, those of working age not being able to come before the actual class. There is the occasional nod from one or another of them, which he returns, but no words. He knows none of their names. The mood of these pre-class sessions is always quiet, focused. He practices his stances, feeling in tune with the mood of the others.

This evening though he feels something different in himself, something cleaner, as if the view from his window as he'd listened to the bells or the smooth flow of ink as he'd written the sutra had rinsed out a fouled conduit in his mind. As he goes through the strange stances rounding the Circle of Eight he feels himself flowing rather than changing, and when he pauses in one or another of the stances he feels as if he is still flowing rather than pausing. He no longer is concentrating, does not need to concentrate. He simply flows. He is aware of the arrival of each of the later students, but not distracted by them. When Terayama arrives and then reappears in uniform and the class lines up and bows and sits into meditation, West is still flowing, flowing through these actions just as in the exercises. Even in meditation the sense of flowing.

After meditation they work the circles individually, holding the mind of meditation in the stances, which today for him is still just the flow, and then when they pair for their odd way of sparring he still flows. Terayama always assigns the pairs. West begins with a man in his forties, perhaps the third or fourth most senior of the class. They circle. West flows. He has no idea how long this match has gone on when Terayama calls Stop. He knows he has heard the thumps as juniors have fallen to Already Hit, and it occurs to him that he has not fallen.

He is paired next with the second most senior of the class, and again he flows and hears the thumps and cries as juniors take their falls and again he is surprised when Terayama calls Stop and he has not fallen.

For his third match he is paired with the most senior of the class and again he flows. He notices that his opponent is subtly reducing the diameter of their circle, yet he continues to flow. Suddenly the man shouts and attacks with a blow to his solar plexus. Terayama shouts Stop.

All right, Kansen-gobosan, he says. You have successfully defended against Already hit. But you forgot this is still karate, didn't you? Again.

So he goes through several more pairs, starting with the most senior and working down the ranks. The three most senior nail him again, the same way, with conventional karate, not with Already Hit. The fourth tries it, but West is able to block and counterpunch. With his equals and juniors he can flow and still can win the conventional matches, but has not learned yet how to impose Already Hit on his opponents, has no idea how that is done.

After class Terayama is clearly pleased with him. Good, Kansen-gobosan, good. Threw the Punch is harder than Already Hit, but perhaps it will be easier now. The defense is the most important part. Very few ever learn how to make the attack.

て

He opens his window after his meal and sticks his head out to sniff the cool damp of late March. The plums bloom white, happy to be announcing the renewal of spring, each flower a smile. Children laugh, their mothers natter under their colorful umbrellas.

With a sigh he gathers the tray, carries it to the sliding door and leaves it just outside. Closes the door. Waits until he hears the door downstairs unlock, hears the soft shuffle of feet mounting the stairs, the rustle of cloth and faint clatter of a wooden bowl or chopstick as the tray is lifted, the soft shuffle again as feet retrace the stairs, the solid clank as the downstairs door is relocked. He sighs again. No doubt there is virtue in this absolute sameness of each day, but he finds it impossible to recognize.

Monk's robe, inkstone, brush, sutra. He has had it all memorized for some time, now copies it only for the calligraphic values of the characters, working only to render them in the style of the example, one from a famous Heian period temple in Kyoto. Some of the more complicated of them he despairs of mastering. Well, it seems he will have forever to keep trying.

He draws hard on his memories of Hanako's lessons, but he cannot make them apply here. Instead he finds himself engulfed in pictures of her, meditating, at the calligraphy table, her brush flowing above the paper in some other world, at one with the high spiritual art of sacred calligraphy. He wonders how she can do this and on the same day can wear a thong and stilettos and then dress like an American whore and practice heretical tantric sex, how she is able to move somehow from tawdriness to the sublime, seamlessly and with no apparent difficulty or sense of contradiction. She can do this, he decides, because her mind is completely undisturbed. He is sure she lives on a plane beyond concern for mere forms.

He, however, does not, cannot. He gives up on the sutra and cleans the brush and inkstone and goes back to the window and sighs again. He watches the mists move and change their patterns over the mountains, breathes in the rain-washed city air and longs to walk in those mountains and breathe their air instead. Again he sighs. Spring fever. Cabin fever.

He knows he could escape. He could overpower the person who brings the meal or whomever collects the tray and make a dash for the downstairs door. He could even pack his kit, have it ready for when he made his run.

But he knows he will not, that if he did that he could never come back, could not even return to Takamatsu. He will see this through, all the way through.

But some days he simply can't appreciate it.

Heaving yet another sigh he begins again to grind ink. He wishes he had a big brush, big sheets of paper, so he could write broadly, wildly, rather than have to work within the confines of the tiny sutra characters. Today, rather than copying, he writes the sutra several times from memory in a grassy abbreviated script, as fast as he can. He doesn't care how it looks when he's finished. Even this does not really help. He again cleans his brush and inkstone and lies down on the tatami mat, cradles his head with a sitting cushion, closes his eyes and visualizes a path through those misted mountains.

But there is no path. There are winding patterns of low grasses among the trees and undergrowth, seeming to lead nowhere. He stands lost, has no idea which way to go. He hears the approach of his pursuers and so begins to run, simply away from the sounds, choosing one winding track after another, any route that seems to lead away from them. Branches reach for his clothing, brush clings to his legs. He runs and runs. Tiring he pauses, listens. He hears them no more.

As he stands there he notices a fox in the brush, watching him. The fox moves tentatively into an open patch, still watching him intently. The fox does not speak, but he knows it is telling him to follow, that it will lead him away to safety.

He decides to trust the fox and when he does the fox turns and trots ahead in a new direction. Branches no longer claw, brush no longer clings. The way leads upward into rocky terrain, outcroppings, boulders, crevasses. His progress slows. The fox often pauses to look back over its shoulder at him. The pace is hard and he hears himself breathing heavily.

The fox leads him into a sort of grotto formed by fallen rock. He sees the fox's tail as it disappears into a tiny crease in the rock where surely he cannot follow. He turns around to find a way out, a way back, perhaps, though where back might be he does not know.

Suddenly he hears shuffling and heavy breath and then feels himself gripped from behind by powerful arms. He can see that the arms are human and belong to more than one person. He hears panting and grunts and guttural, unfamiliar words in Japanese. Then he is blindfolded and bound and half-carried for some distance, struggling. He feels himself forced down into the Lotus position and bound to something that locks him there. He hears the slither of cloth, feels himself draped in it, some sort of garment.

He begins to panic, foreknowing what is happening to

him. The blindfold is removed. He sees that he is on a sort of platform, in a small cave. He sees that he is draped in an ornate brocade of red silk shot with gold, the very robe worn by the monk at the waterfall and by all of the mummies of the Senkyo temple. He dimly sees figures at work outside, fitting a stone over the opening of the cave. The fox looks in at him through what is left of the opening, then turns itself into a woman wearing a Noh mask and kimono. She emits a long, quavering word he doesn't understand. He wakes to this sound rising from his own throat.

He prepares himself mechanically for evening meditation and karate, but the dream impinges, its images recur. He leaves the window open all the while, often stopping to stare at the distant mountains. Who were his pursuers? Could the fox who turned into a woman be anyone other than Hanako? Has she somehow been betraying him, or is he just so lonely that he feels betrayed? Although he has dreamed, or recalled dreams, seldom since being in Japan, those he has had have played out in waking life in ways they never have before. He thinks of the souvenir shop, the pool, the bronze of the Kappa. And this is the second appearance of the fox and the figure in the Noh mask. How might these images someday appear in life awake?

Students begin to arrive. He joins them in the warm-up postures, but finds himself more attentive now to the other students, feeling something close to suspicion of them. Are they his pursuers? Are they among those who would bind him and bury him alive? Had he heard their derisive laughter as the figures sealed the cave?

These thoughts persist despite his efforts to regain control of his mind until meditation actually begins. Through it he settles, finds emptiness, and can sustain it as they practice the forms. But when it comes time for pairs the thoughts return. He hates and fears each opponent he faces, senior or junior to him. In each match his ferocity is turned against him and he is bruised, cracked, wrenched by blows and falls. Finally the most senior student uses Threw the Punch to move in and knock him unconscious.

When he revives the man helps him to the wall and seats him on his heels, waves a finger in his face, then presents his flattened palm. He is to sit in place until told otherwise. This lasts until the class aligns itself for closing meditation, when Terayama signs to him to take his position, now at the very back. Not a word when meditation ends and all leave. He remains sitting, buried in shame even as he struggles for emptiness.

In the morning it is as usual, though during sword class he feels some apprehension about his private lesson with Terayama. No one in the class behaves any differently toward him, and mind and sword and body blend correctly despite his aches and pains. But when all but he and Terayama have left they do not take to the Circle of Eights as usual. Terayama beckons him into the small room, sits formally, and tells West to sit before him.

So, Terayama says, as for last night, what?

West, having spoken to no one for so long, finds it difficult to begin.

Today you may speak, Kansen-gobosan. West nods.

Still it is difficult. Terayama waits patiently, unmoving, expressionless. West raises his eyes to him at last.

I was looking at the mountains, and then I slept and of them had a dream. It was a dream of being pursued and caught and buried alive. The dream stayed with me, and I was afraid that those in the class were those who pursued me in my dream. Out of fear I fought desperately.

Terayama looks down, appears to ponder. It is a long time before he speaks.

For young monks to have strong dreams is not unusual, especially in the silent and lonely periods of their training. How your mind chased thoughts when you were first learning to meditate, do you remember?

Yes, Sensei.

And your first teacher of meditation, what did he say about them?

That they were not important. That one should simply let them dissipate.

Good. We think of dreams exactly as we think of such thoughts. They have no importance in our practice.

Yes, Sensei.

So you followed your dream instead of letting it go, as you were taught to let go of thoughts in meditation, didn't you?

Yes, Sensei.

Don't do that again, Kansen-gobosan. What if you were actually fighting for your life? It is true that the sword and meditation are the same thing. But what happens in meditation in the end is more important than the life or death which might occur under the sword. It takes much of a lifetime to learn that. This is the reason the Senkyo Sect studies the sword and meditation together. You must bring the same quality of concentration to both. Meditate as if you were fighting with live swords, and fight as if you were calmly meditating.

Yes, Sensei.

They sit silently. Birdsong gradually fills the room, wrens, West thinks, nesting. Terayama's eyes turn to the open window, seeming to rest in the soft shapes of the distant peaks.

While looking at the mountains you wanted to walk in them? Terayama says.

Yes, Sensei.

Of course you did. It is spring. I look at them now and I too want to walk in them.

He falls silent again, the distance in his eyes expanding beyond any mere view of mountain or forest, beyond any place defined only by space but now filled with time. It seems some minutes before he sighs and closes those eyes and turns back to West with a fleeting smile crossing withered lips.

But neither of us can go to walk in the mountains quite yet. Soon though, I promise. Not too much longer. You are almost there, Kansen-gobosan. Truly, almost there. Please persevere.

Through the open window he smells flowers, though when he looks out he can't see them, sees just the moonlit roof tiles and the chiaroscuro of the plums in full leaf and the outlines of the mountains beyond. It is June again.

Meditation, sword class, karate. After all the others have left, Terayama pauses at the door to speak to him. The old man has shrunk and wizened and darkened to a deep yellow brown and seems very weak. His voice is shaky, but clear enough.

We are finished here, he says. Pack all of your things, and wear clothes for travel, shoes for hiking. Don't forget your sutras. I will return for you in an hour.

The first nine months dragged on and on, but now, as he is packing to leave, the year as a whole seems to have flown. He remembers how in March he wanted only to flee this place, and is surprised that today he finds he dreads leaving it. Clocks and calendars have become irrelevant. He has lived without either for a year, depending on the bells for the time, and the temperature and views from his window for the seasons. He has learned so much. He has become, he thinks, Kansen, and is West no more.

And he remembers having packed for a few days a year ago. Now he packs the same things, having added his monk's robe and a roll of sutras. He has never needed the wooden sandals. Perhaps he will in this next phase.

As he dresses in western clothes for the first time in a year he gives a thought to how he will appear out in public. Although he has shaved his face every day, he realizes that he has done nothing with his hair and that it falls now well past his shoulders. How will that look? He shrugs.

He is finished and ready, and waits for some time in the vestibule. He has already donned and fastened his split-toed cloth laborer's boots. He stands, walks a few steps down and back up the stairs to test them. They feel all right, but odd. His whole costume feels odd. He has worn no shoes and only his robe and uniforms for a full year.

He hears the lock of the downstairs door clanking, watches the pale daylight from the covered street climb the stairs. Sees Terayama's silhouette formed by it.

Hurry up, the old man says.

West bows, collects his bag, hustles down the stairs. Bows again, helps close the door. Terayama doesn't bother to lock it.

Horse already left barn, he says.

There is a taxi stand on a main street less than a block away. One has its Occupied light on. They get in it, and the driver pulls away without a word being said, takes them straight to the station.

On the way Terayama whispers, Buy a ticket to Tosaguchi. It is a very small station in the mountains. You will know it because there is a big white hotel up the slope to the west. Don't go there. Go across the tracks. There is a small village not far to the east. It has one open-front tea house. Eat there, sit and wait. I will be there about an hour later. When you see me pass on the street, follow me. If anyone asks, you are going to hike to Osugi.

Yes, Sensei.

He does as he is told. The train labors often on the rises, the country gets steadily rougher, higher, with less and less evidence of civilization, even of agriculture. There are few people aboard, all dressed for the city. None get off at any of the minor stops.

He steps down onto a tiny, empty platform high in the green, steep mountains. Tosaguchi. The entrance to the old name of the prefecture he is in, now called Kochi-ken. He is the only passenger to get off there. He stands alone in the rain, listening to the train fade off to the south. When it is gone, the quiet is overwhelming.

He turns his face to the high slopes behind them. He does not want to move, just to take in the air, which is moist and unbearably clean, now that the stink of the train has dispersed. It is much cooler here than on the coastal plain he's just left, almost cold. Rich in greens, shrouded in soft white mists, clouds hovering around the peaks like spirits. Oh yes, beautiful indeed, marred only by the western-style hotel spoiling the view to the west.

He turns east and crosses the tracks and finds the village and the tea house. The front is open despite the rain. A carved wooden black badger grins over his bright red painted erection. The old wood beams are darkened by smoke, the dense thatch drips softly. It is dark within, no tatami, low tables with polished tree stumps for chairs.

A wrinkled elderly woman wears a gray kimono and white apron and welcomes him, asks him what he might want. He finds he truly is hungry. He orders soba with seaweed and sips tea until it comes. It is delicious. He lingers, orders more tea.

After a while he sees the old man walking by. He moves slowly, with small steps but a straight back. He carries a long hiking staff, and has a package wrapped in a blue cloth slung from it. West pays the bill and follows him at a leisurely pace, taking in the sights of the village, which seem to consist mainly of curio shops. He stops to admire a wooden fox, a Noh mask, a large dragon-carved inkstone. No one speaks to him.

They follow the paved road out of the village. Once past the village the road is no longer paved, and gradually reduces itself to a path. When even the outlying cottages are out of sight Terayama waves him forward.

We will be leaving Tosa, actually, he says. We go into Tokushima Prefecture, though I think of these as still being the Tosa mountains. Well, we have a long walk, Kansen-gobosan. Let's go.

Then they continue, always upward, no matter how the paths twist and turn amidst the tall conifers. The rocks are greenish, the mosses a great range of rust orange, yellows, almost blue greens. Small waterfalls pour the remnants of snows above not fully melted. Tiny birds flit joyously around them. A squirrel scolds them for disrupting his afternoon.

They cover several kilometers this way, with all the twists and turns West has no idea how many. Near evening they come upon an isolated cottage with a thatched roof, almost hidden in gorse and pine. Terayama walks up to the door and calls out. There is no response. He calls twice more, then slides open the unlocked wooden door. They peer into the gloom. No one.

They sit on the stoop under the thatch and remove their boots. When Terayama steps up he totters. He goes inside, lies down on the browned, torn tatami mat. I am tired, Kansen-gobosan, he says. Very tired.

Can I do anything for you, Sensei?

See if there is water, fuel to boil it for tea, please.

Yes, Sensei.

He sees that there is a stone-framed hole in the tatami with ashes in it. He looks in the various closets, finds a kettle and cups. On a shelf in another he finds a hemp sack with chopped charcoal in it, some candles, a small box of wooden matches. Further searching reveals no paper, no pump or stored water.

Pardon me, Sensei. Is there a well?

I don't know. Out behind the house there will be water nearby.

Yes, Sensei.

He takes the kettle, puts on his wooden sandals, and goes out to search. The rain has stopped but the fog is heavy, the air is chill in the twilight. He moves slowly on the leveled gravel surrounding the house. He scans the underbrush, the mossy outcrops, the low branches. He does not want to see a fox. He is uneasy with the noise his wooden sandals make on the gravel, stops often to listen to the forest. He turns the corner and follows the narrow line of gravel along the back of the house. A small animal scurries from under the flooring and flees into the gorse, shocking him.

But there is a cistern, a large wooden bucket under inverted tiles still slowly dripping. Hung on a wooden peg on its side is a bamboo ladle. The bucket is overflowing. With the kettle filled he returns the way he came. Too dark now to explore the other side of the house. At the stoop he slips out of his wooden sandals, moves cautiously into the dark room.

May I light a candle, Sensei?

No answer. There is no choice. He feels around the open closet for the matches and finds them, finds a candle, lights it. Dips some wax from it onto the shelf and sticks it there. He goes over to Terayama, kneels by his side.

Sensei? Do you still want tea? he whispers.

But Terayama is breathing heavily and evenly, almost snoring. So he quietly fishes his roll of sutras out of his pack, takes three of his scribbled, cursive copies and crumples them into the fire space, arranges charcoal over them. Then he finds some bedding, covers Terayama, makes up a bed for himself.

Doesn't lie in it. He blows out the candle and kneels on the tatami mat and recites the sutra silently. And then silently converses with an imaginary Terayama.

Sensei, why travel together could we not?

Because I'm taking you to a place where no foreigner has ever been before.

But, why not together?

It is a secret place.

Sensei, my Special Assignment. It's because of that, isn't it?

Yes, Kansen-gobosan. This is the first phase of that.

West lies down then and loosens his clothes and covers himself. He listens to scurrying noises in the thatch for some time before he sleeps.

छ

West is awakened by the smell of scented charcoal. Terayama has started the fire and has put the kettle on the coals and has lit a candle. The old man sits watching the coals. He appears to be meditating.

West rises and goes to the door, opens it quietly, puts on his wooden sandals and steps out into the forest to relieve himself. It is still full dark and chilly and damp. He listens to the forest but hears only his stream. He steps back onto the gravel and with a hand on the coarsely planked wall guides himself to the cistern and by feel finds the ladle and pours the cold water over his head and rubs his eyes. When he returns the kettle is boiling, but Terayama sits as before. West sits across from him.

You used your sutras for kindling, Terayama says.

Yes, Sensei. But only some scribbled ones.

The most sacred of them, perhaps.

About this I don't know.

It is all right. There is a tradition of burning holy paper, as a message to the Buddhas. I prayed for our success as they burned.

Terayama takes some leaves or herbs from his cloth package, then digs deeper, finds something else. I brought some buckwheat for our tea.

Thank you, Sensei.

Terayama pulls a plastic flask out of his package. Fill this with the leftover water, he says. West does so.

They drink their tea and make sure the fire is out and tidy the cottage and set off again, light just a gray idea in the east. They trudge up the path, Terayama leading, moving very slowly. A strong smell of wet pine permeates the air. Small animals rustle the brush. Birds flit reluctantly from branches. Only when the eastern sky turns red do they begin to chirp. A chill breeze rises. Dew on the grass underfoot soaks through West's cloth boots.

Where path divides and a tree has fallen, Terayama mutters that they have lost the way, have to turn back. An hour or so later they come to another fork. Terayama takes the left one. The sky has gone from red to gold, warming them now, drying West's feet. In another half an hour Terayama shakes his head, says, No. Mistake, mistake. Turns back, spots a smaller path, turns again. West is now certain he can never find his way back alone.

At what must be noon they hear the seven spaced booms of a distant low-pitched bell. Ah, Terayama says. That is the bell of the Senkyo temple. We are going the right way. Let us stop and eat something.

With the sun at its zenith the air has warmed, West's feet are dry at last. They sit in a grassy clearing. Terayama draws the flask of water from his pack, offers it to West, who takes a sip and uses a few drops to clean his hands. Terayama does the same. They recite the brief chant before meals. He then takes out a small paper packet, unfolds it. It contains a variety of nuts. He offers them to West.

Take the dark ones, he says. Not too bitter.

West thinks as he chews that they must be chestnuts or something related. They share the packet, Terayama eating the lighter-colored ones, West the darker. When it is empty Terayama folds the paper and replaces it in his sack. It has been very little food. They sip a little more water, then they recite the sutra for after meals.

We cannot rest long, Terayama says. Still a long way to go.

The old man has difficulty rising. West bends, puts a hand under an elbow, picks up both packs and hands him his staff. He nods curtly in thanks.

Late afternoon. Clouds are building in the west. A wind rises gradually, a gusty, twisting wind that is whipping branches by the time they reach the place. It is a tiny clearing under a huge cedar, surrounded by low underbrush which makes it invisible from what little there is of a path. Terayama leads him through an opening barely big enough for rabbits. He goes to the great tree, rubs its bark with his palm, smiling. Then he leads him around the tree to a ragged cliff behind. There he points out a crevasse behind some shrubs that appears to form the entrance to a cave. West sees a triangular wooden structure recessed into it, covered with dead pine branches and living vines. Terayama goes up to it, tugs at one side of it. Some dirt and pine needles fall, but it does not move.

Help me, Kansen-gobosan.

West drops the packs and walks forward. He sees where Terayama has tried to move the structure, which he now sees is a door. He pulls. After initial resistance it swings easily outward, hung on oddly shaped hinges. Behind it is a tiny A-shaped cave. A stone floor has been swept out and stripped of any vegetation intruding on the inside. Another wooden A-shape, not a meter in, forms the back of the little room.

This, what is it? he asks.

A private meditation place, the old man tells him as he walks away. When you are finished looking, close the door please.

West stares into the space and shivers as a gust of wind rattles the pines. A child of four could barely stand in it. It was meant for a much smaller person.

He closes the door and joins Terayama under the great cedar, where he finds him sitting silently, watching the rain clouds coming over the distant peaks and ridges. He sits with him, not speaking. Sheets of sunlight find them, leave them. The wind seems to chase the sunlit patches, always striking only shadow. Tiny sparrows fly back and forth from the lower limbs of the tree to a bush laden with small red berries. They don't sing, seem to be keeping an eye on the building clouds. As the late sun falls behind them it turns chill again. They sit for a long time. The colors, first bright silvers and golds and then pinks and then reds gradually deepen into purple and mauve. Only when the sun has set does Terayama pick up his staff and rise. Without a word he begins to walk downhill toward the west.

West follows him, stumbling often in the near dark, grateful now for the old man's slow pace. They drop into a stand of willows, wet their feet in the trickle of a stream, climb again. When they climb out of there and can again see the sky it is bordered by the outline of a cluster of buildings against the faint last suggestion of twilight under the cloud bank. He hears thunder flat and dull in the distance, and a misty rain starts to fall.

Nearing the buildings he can make out a wall. Terayama alters his course slightly, bearing right. The wall appears blank, but this turn leads them to a small gate, a sort of hatch they have to bend almost double to enter. A small garden, West thinks. Anyway another walled space with a building beyond it. A door. Terayama slides it open.

I commit a discourtesy, Terayama says, bowing deeply. A voice from within says Welcome. A silhouette appears.

Step up, the shadow says. They rise, enter the vestibule and bow. Welcome, welcome, Reikyo-hoshi. Come in, come in.

Leaving their packs in the vestibule, they remove their shoes and step up into a bare four- and a-half mat room. In the low light of a small oil lamp West sees a wrinkled old man who bows and with a gesture invites them to sit, then seats himself at a small writing table. On it is a book of sutras he has been reading. Terayama introduces West as Kansen, and their host simply as Soincho.

The two old men converse quietly, rather formally. Terayama is always addressed as Hoshi, their host always as Soincho. West listens, following most of it, but he is nodding, blinking. He feels certain that there is a layer of meaning beneath the talk of how things are going in Takamatsu and at the dojo in Zentsuji, about the trains and the village of Tosaguchi, but he cannot guess what that meaning might be. He can see that Terayama is fading too. Finally the soincho seems to take notice.

You must be tired, he says. I will show you to your quarters.

The soincho rises easily, taking up the oil lamp. West is stiff, but Terayama is having a hard time of it. West begins to offer a hand but the old man refuses it silently. Once they are upright West collects their packs and the soincho leads them down a hall to another four- and a-half mat room. West drops their packs in a corner, sees that beneath a small wooden Buddha there is lamp in the rudimentary shrine. He turns to the abbot for permission to light it, and receives a nod.

As he is lighting it the soincho says, In the morning Kansen will go out through the private gate and go back up to the willows. Sendo-gobosan will meet him there and lead him to the front, where he will beg to become a monk. The guard will send him to the front door of this building, and I will accept him. He will be assigned a mat and given his bowls. Sendo-gobosan will teach him the proper way to eat, make up his bedding, all that. Shave his head. At this, both the soincho and Terayama run palms over their bald heads and smile like two old friends.

Sleep well, the abbot says. He bows slightly and with-draws, closing the paper door.

West looks in the cabinet, finds only rudimentary bedding. Terayama has already stretched out on the tatami mats and closed his eyes. West covers him, asks if he wants a pillow.

No, Kansen-gobosan. This will be fine.

West takes a pillow and a small cover and picks a corner away from Terayama and the packs, then blows out the lamp and lies down and sleeps almost instantly.

き

Morning in darkness. Terayama has lit the lamp and leads him down the hall to a toilet first, then to a washroom where they clean themselves in cold water. They return to their room. Terayama replaces the lamp under the Buddha in the shrine, sits and bows. West does the same. Then they simply meditate.

It is a long period of meditation, much longer than they'd ever done even in the Zentsuji dojo. It is still dark when Terayama claps his hands, bows, and chants the Four Vows Sutra. As they chant they hear the peal of the great bell, a rich, powerful bell even though muffled because of the closed room. When it has finished its four strokes Terayama continues to sit.

You may stretch your legs now, he says.

West rises and does a series of stretches, wondering why Terayama does not join him. Life gradually returns to his legs. He stretches his upper body as well. He feels fresh and calm apart from his concern for his teacher.

Sit now, Terayama says, turning himself to face into the room. West sits formally facing him.

This morning you will become a Senkyo Temple monk, Terayama says. You will be the first and probably the only foreigner ever to do so.

Yes, Sensei. It is a great honor.

Terayama does not respond to this. From now on, you will say Hoshi, not Sensei.

Yes, Hoshi.

You will live with the other monks, exactly as they live. You will not think of the future, because everything here exists outside of time. You will have monk's food and monk's work. You will stay deep within yourself. You will discover there your true nature, and the nature of Nature.

Yes, Hoshi. Then he cannot help asking, Will I see you again?

Yes. But none of the other monks will know I am here, and you must not tell any of them.

Yes, Hoshi, West says, wanting desperately to ask why but knowing he cannot.

Go now. Be a good monk.

Yes, Hoshi. Sayonara.

Terayama bows slightly, waves him off.

He gathers his things and takes his pack and finds his way in the dark back to the soincho's room, which is dimly lit. The soincho is in deep meditation there, does not look up. West quietly slides the door open, closes it, sits on the stoop and pulls on his still-damp split-toed boots. He leaves silently.

Once he is past the garden and out through the hatch in the wall, he can see the willows silhouetted by a pinking dawn. They are not far away. He walks toward them as quickly as he can in the scanty light. The air is cool and intensely fresh. The grass is still damp underfoot. Memories of such mornings in his youth at home appear, tempt him to reverie, to an imaginary revel in childhood. Then the question, Who was I then? and its inevitable companion, Who am I now? With an effort he allows all this to flow past, and is rewarded by the scent of some flower or herb he's never before encountered. Oh, it's good to be alive.

He enters the stand of willows and the scent here is of

dank earth. There is now enough light that he can see to hop across the little stream. He follows the path upward, scanning for the monk who is to meet him there. Birds begin to sing as they fly in whirring passages from branch to branch. Oh, what a morning.

Just as the last of the trees are behind him a voice calls, Kansen-gobosan. Stop.

He stops. The voice has come from somewhere to his left and behind him. He becomes aware of the smell of charcoal burning, realizes the faint breeze has carried it away from him until now.

Come, the voice says. Sit with me.

West turns slowly toward the voice. He sees a man in a brown monk's robe sitting crosslegged on the ground under one of the last willows. A square of soaked cloth is spread across its lower branches, protecting the man from the dew. He wears a pair of straw sandals tied with ropes around high, white, split-toed socks. Before him a small charcoal fire sends a wisp of smoke up and around a tiny kettle. The man offers a half a smile, beckons him over. He walks the few paces to the man, bows.

Sendo I am, he says, bowing slightly from his seat.

West I am.

No. You are Kansen-gobosan. Sit.

West drops to his knees and sits formally. So now I am Kansen, he thinks. Once I was West, now I am Kansen. Of course.

Sendo drops a handful of seeds into the kettle, replaces the lid, moves the pot away from the fire. We will have tea, he says. It will be a few hours before we can go to the gate.

Kansen again wants to ask why, but dares not. All this secrecy. He shrugs inwardly, says just Thank you.

Reikyo-hoshi, he is with the soincho?

That no one is supposed to know, Kansen says.

Good. A secret, neh? Only the soincho and I know. And you.

Again he wants to ask why, but dares not.

I had to know, because otherwise I would wonder and the other monks would wonder.

I understand, he says, but he doesn't. Last night, you slept out? he asks.

Two nights.

The rain?

A cave I know. Pleasant, it was, to meditate in the cave with the sound of the rain.

Sendo leans forward to twirl and test the teapot. As he does, Kansen looks closely at him. His face is long and narrow and deeply lined, and Kansen guesses he is about fifty. He is slim, but his movements, even from his seated position, are smooth and athletic.

So, Reikyo-hoshi has brought you here to become a monk.

This is so, I think.

You do not know?

There is something else, perhaps.

Just become a monk.

Yes, Hoshi.

Gobosan, no more.

Yes, Gobosan. Then after a long silence Kansen asks, Gobosan, can you tell me some things?

What?

Please, what does Soincho mean?

Soin means monastery. Soincho means boss of the monastery. What do you say in English?

Abbot.

Yes.

And what do gobosan and hoshi mean?

Gobosan is how you address priests. Seniors like Reikyo get Hoshi. It means Teacher of the Dharma.

Thank you. I understand. And your name?

Do, Salvation. Same Sen as yours.

Thank you, Gobosan.

Sendo decides that the tea is ready, pulls two small cups from his pack and pours. They bow their heads and whisper I receive from above me, and sip. It is buckwheat tea, warm and earthy and delicious.

Gobosan, would you teach me about the temple? It is all secret?

It takes Sendo some time to answer. When he does, Kansen hears some careful reluctance in his voice.

Few people know about it, but how can it be secret? There are satellites, neh?

He pauses again, obviously considering what more he can say.

It is of the Rinzai Zen Sect, the branch of Myoshinji in Kyoto, but it is officially considered part of the little temple you attended in Takamatsu. The priest there answers to Myoshinji. He never comes here. Myoshinji has over three thousand affiliated temples. They take no interest in us at all. So we are a sort of open secret.

I didn't know we were of the Zen Sect.

We were not, until the occupation. When we left Mount Koya entirely and all moved here, we were only Senkyo Sect. Not until after that did we come under Rinzai.

So, please, how does the temple sustain itself?

On donations from certain rich people.

Like Yamazaki Industries?

Sendo shoots him a hooded glance, holds it for a moment, then looks off to the east.

Like them, yes. We grow our own vegetables for pickling, and our own buckwheat for tea. Stores of rice and dried seaweed, oil for the stoves and lamps, a few other things, are trucked in twice a year. We need very little.

The sun rises into a clear washed sky, warming and drying them. Birds flit and sing. A rabbit emerges from the brush under the willows, stares at them for a full minute, then nibbles grasses. Sendo lies back, stretches his legs and stares up at the drying cloth. Following his lead, Kansen too lies back and stretches his legs and closes his eyes against the brightness. The rabbit starts at their movements, takes a few hops away, then calmly continues his munching. The next hours pass in companionable silence, both men drifting in and out of sleep.

ゆ

It is nearly mid-morning when Sendo sits up, rubs his eyes.

Now we can go, he says. He rises and takes down the sun-dried cloth from the branches and begins to pack his things into it. Kansen stands and stretches, picks up his kit. They then head back into the willows and across the little stream and then turn right and soon join a wider, more definite path downhill toward the monastery. This path soon joins a two-rutted road with gravel spread over the low spots, a vehicle track. And in a short time they pass the eastern wall and come to the main gate.

A young monk sits on a bench beside the great wooden gate. The gate is open. Kansen can see the abbot's quarters just to the left, and the main temple building farther in, past an open space crisscrossed by flagstone walkways. To the left is what may be the bathhouse and toilets. Beyond that he can see part of another building. All are wattled and the color of adobe and roofed in nearly black tiles.

The young monk stands. Welcome back, Sendo-gobosan, he says bowing. When he straightens he looks at Kansen, shows a flash of surprise and curiosity at seeing a foreigner.

This is Kansen-gobosan, Sendo says. Reikyo-hoshi has sent him from Zentsuji to become a monk, if the abbot will have him.

Kansen and the young monk bow and mutter Pleased to

meet you for the first time. Then Sendo motions Kansen to follow him. They walk to the entrance of the abbot's quarters, where Sendo tells Kansen to kneel and bury his face. Then he calls out I commit a discourtesy. The door slides open and the abbot appears.

Sendo says it all again, that Kansen has been sent by Reikyo-hoshi from Zentsuji, but this time in higher, more formal language that Kansen can hardly follow. They speak at some length this way, with Kansen curled up, his face in the sand. At last the abbot says Get up, Kansen-gobosan, and the ceremony, all pre-planned, is over.

Sendo-gobosan leads him to a well next to the bathhouse and has him kneel and sit formally. He then goes around to the back of the bathhouse and returns in a moment. He pulls scissors out of the left sleeve of his robe, shortens Kansen's long hair to a stubble. He then douses his head with water from a dipper and soaps it, takes out a plastic safety razor and shaves his head completely. Another brief rinse and it is done.

He realizes that he should feel some apprehension at what is happening to him, but does not. He is filled with enthusiasm for the waiting adventure. He follows Sendo-gobosan then to the toilet, where he changes from his cotton clothing into the long brown robe, belts it with the black sash, and puts on his wooden sandals. Sendo watches all this closely, examines him critically when he is finished. Then he smiles.

Good, he says. Kansen is now a true monk.

Then he puts the western clothes and split-toed boots in Kansen's pack and runs with it toward the abbot's quarters. He meets Kansen near the well in less than two minutes.

The order is largely a silent one, a rule seldom broken, Sendo tells him. So do not talk unless I ask you a question.

Yes Gobosan.

The rest of the morning's instruction includes only the

rare, whispered word from Sendo-gobosan, nods only from Kansen. He is issued bedding, three bowls and a pair of chopsticks, and led to the main hall. He finds a small inkstone, water bottle and paperweight on the small table in the sliding compartment in the wall above his mat. He is shown how to lay out the bedding for sleep, how to re-fold it and store it in the sliding compartment. Sendo-gobosan then takes out the table and bowls from behind the mat next to them, shows him how to bow in thanks, ask for food, refuse more food. Then in a whisper, he describes how to leave one Takuan pickle at the end to use to clean out the bowls. When they are clean, to eat the pickle. Then the bowls are to be rubbed with the tiny cotton napkin included in the stack. The lot goes back into the compartment, exactly so.

Sendo-gobosan takes him on a small tour. The altar in the hall is a larger version of the one in Takamatsu, but not in the Zen style. There is a statue of the Dainichi Buddha, very old and weathered, as if it has spent a century or two exposed to the elements. Around to the left and behind it is a room for private consultation, plain, with only a scroll in the shrine, of the single character, Emptiness. They sit and watch the scroll for a few moments, then Sendo-gobosan opens the sliding door at the back of the room, motions him to come and look.

Behind it, on a kind of throne, a mummy sits in a perfect Lotus position, back straight, eyes closed, or so it seems in the dim light, hands cupped in a circle and resting peacefully on the lap. The skin is patchy brown parchment. It is dressed in a simple monk's robe, very old and worn, with a second one, quite new, of shiny gold and red silk draped over the shoulders. Though the mouth is somewhat torn, exposing a few teeth, the expression is one of gentle peace, the truly carefree mind.

After they have looked long at the mummy, Sendo-gobosan quietly closes the sliding door. Living Buddha, he whispers. The first ever Senkyo. Now he is Senkyo-kai. Once someone has made a Buddha in this living body, he is called kai instead of hoshi.

Kansen kneels and bows deeply at the closed door.

They step outside into bright sunlight. Sendo leads him to the toilets, shows him the outdoor baths. As they are walking back toward the remaining outbuildings he has not yet been shown the bell begins to ring, the most beautiful bell Kansen has ever heard. When he had heard it in the morning it had a beautiful sound, true, but not like this, right here within ten meters of it. It echoes and bounces, soaring around the surrounding hills, a great bird in flight, each new stroke a fresh dream riding above the echoes.

They stop to watch the monks ring it. The process is the same as at New Years in Takamatsu, except that there are only seven monks for seven strokes. From where Kansen stands he can see their lips move in a short prayer, which might or might not be silent; only the praying monk would ever know. After descending from the platform, each monk in turn walks toward the main temple.

Sendo signals Kansen to follow. They enter the main temple, go to their respective mats. Many are already sitting with their bowls and chopsticks and cloths aligned before them, meditating. Kansen copies Sendo's actions, sits as he does, drops his hands into a circle in his lap, meditates. Soon the last of the monks has settled. The abbot appears from behind the altar, sits, and begins the Sutra Before the Meal. All join in.

As the last phrase falls to silence, monks enter carrying cauldrons, and spoon out measures of brown rice, buckwheat tea, pickles and vegetables. The serving monks come around a second time. All but two or three refuse seconds with a formal hand gesture. Most of the old men refuse rice, draw nuts and leaves from small pouches like Terayama carries. Each monk finishes his meal, washes his bowls with the Takuan pickle and eats it, stacks the bowls and returns them to their sliding compartments and then resumes meditation until all have finished. At that point the abbot leads the Sutra After the Meal, and all meditate for some twenty more minutes. During the sutra chanting, Kansen observes the postures of the other monks. Some sit formally as he does, some of the older monks in full or half Lotus.

The abbot strikes the wooden blocks, ending the session. The monks stretch their legs, then stand on the planked aisles, waiting. When the blocks clap again the monks begin to walk in a slow and dignified manner, eyes lowered. The line makes a complete circuit of the hall, then the monks file out to the vestibule, slide into their wooden sandals and go silently to their appointed tasks. Just as they do so the bell begins to toll. Eight strokes.

Kansen and Sendo leave in turn. They head toward the back of the compound, where there are several outbuildings. They go to the largest of them.

It is the dojo. Somewhat larger inside than the one in Zentsuji, but much the same except for the rows of shoji windows lining both of its long walls. The wood swords are in racks by the main entrance, and several Circles of Eight are etched in the polished pine floor. Sendo begins opening the shoji screens along the far wall. Kansen does the same on the near one.

He is just starting to slide the next to last screen when he feels it, the beginning of it, he is being attacked with Already Hit. He spins and drops into a deep low stance and raises his hands in guard position. He sees Sendo standing calmly, hands folded in front of his belt, looking at him.

Good, Sendo says. You can defend against Already Hit, even when it's not expected. Very good. Can you also defend against Threw the Punch?

Yes, Gobosan. Sometimes.

All right. Take a sword. Let's see how much of that you remember. We have over an hour before the regular class starts.

They go through the series of memorized sword pairs. It feels familiar and is as much fun as always. Sendo corrects a stance now and then, and adjusts with great precision some of the sword angles, and drills him repeatedly in the various times the right hand is to relax, the left to tighten the grip. Kansen finds this fascinating, delightful. At least an hour passes.

The bell rings, nine strokes this time. Sendo stops, stands at attention. Kansen matches his posture and they move the swords down to the side in the right hand, bow formally.

The regular class starts in a few minutes, Sendo says. Do you have any questions before we go?

Yes, Gobosan. Please, can you tell me, how did Senkyo-kai discover Already Hit and Threw the Punch? In fact, why did he include the martial arts in the Sect's practices at all?

Sendo glares at him, then looks toward the door. How? he says. Why? Short questions. Long answers. Let's go. I will show you the rest of the temple.

They rack their swords and bow to the hall as they reclaim their shoes. As they walk out, several monks are jogging toward the dojo for their class.

Sendo shows him a building in the far southeastern corner near the wall.

That is the clinic, he says. Some of our monks specialize in healing, herbs and acupuncture, moxa and shiatsu. Some of us, usually the youngest and the most elderly, sometimes need treatment for illnesses or injuries.

They walk the other way, toward the west. Here are a series of buildings, some obviously for storage. Sendo points these out, then tells him which is a carpentry shop, a shed for gardening tools and another for lumber and hardware, a smithy. As they walk, he explains the usual schedule of the day.

In the evening, he says, after chanting and meditation, we can use the toilets briefly, and then we go to sleep. The morning bell is very early. You must get up fast, go to the toilet and wash your face and hands, and come back very quickly for chanting and meditation. Then we have one cup of tea, and then it is time for work. Tomorrow you will sweep the walkways until the bell rings six times. Then you will go in and write the sutras until the midday meal. In the afternoon you will help to polish the floors in one of the buildings, and then when the bell rings again, attend karate and sword class. Your duties will change sometimes, but this is how it will go tomorrow.

Yes, Gobosan.

They go out of the compound through a small door cut into a wide gate in the wall to the south. There he shows Kansen the gardens, some forty acres or so, planted with rows of herbs and vegetables and the delicate whites of buckwheat flowers. A few monks are weeding, a few picking early tubers. The field is surrounded by old oaks and young evergreens. Sendo signals him to follow down a path along the edge of the trees. At the farthest end they stop under a spreading grandfather oak. Beyond it is a patch of grasses and wildflowers. Beyond that there are rocks and a cliff rising almost vertically. They sit.

It is because of time, Sendo says once they're settled. His gaze is upward, to the top of the cliff. He stares silently at the empty southern sky.

Kansen waits. And waits. The shadow of an oak branch has time to move across a fold of his robe near his knee to another near his foot before Sendo continues.

Sendo resumes with a question. Can you remember the blow you thought you received the last time you failed to defend against Already Hit?

Kansen thinks.

Yes, he says. It was the same as the punch thrown by Arakawa-sensei that bruised my sternum.

And the time before that?

He thinks. The same punch, he says.

And before that?

Yes. You are right. The same.

And the punch you thought you had thrown the last time you failed to defend against Threw the Punch?

It was the same as the right to the solar plexus I used to defeat Hirano-san in the testing.

And the time before that?

The same punch.

And before that?

Yes. The same.

So, all the same punches every time. Each a punch that happened only once, yes?

Yes, Gobosan.

In the past.

Yes, Gobosan.

And if you had failed to defend against Already Hit just now in the dojo, would it have been the same punch?

Yes, Gobosan.

So it is all concerned with time, past, present, future. Eventually, after being hurt over and over, you learn something about time, don't you? That with Already Hit you remember a punch from the past in a present in which you are not really hit. And that with Threw the Punch you remember a different punch from the past that in the present you have not really thrown yet. What is it you have learned that lets you defend against these techniques?

To stay in the present?

Yes, but more about time in general.

That memory fools you?

Sendo suddenly reaches across and clips him sharply on his newly-shaved head. Idiot! Everyone knows that. Think!

He bows his head and rubs it where it's sore from Sendo's

whack. What does happen? Try to remember. No, that's no good. What do you do to defend against them? Go empty. Sure. But something more. What happens?

Time disappears, he says out loud.

Sendo waits.

But Gobosan, how can time disappear?

Sendo waits some more, staring again at the sky above the cliff. Then says, prompting, Where does time exist?

Kansen stares up there too. Then he laughs. He hears the voice of Ringo Starr, of all people.

It's all in the mind, he says, first in working class Brit English, then in Japanese.

Kansen senses Sendo's smile of approval. They stare together at the top of the cliff, where no cloud floats, no bird flies.

Yes, Sendo says, Time has no reality of its own. Time therefore is elastic. To see what is ultimately real, we must learn to see without believing in time. Also, without believing in space or energy or matter, or anything else we create in our minds. In teaching we start with time, because the belief in time is the easiest habit for the student to break.

But even so, most people never learn this. It takes many years of ordinary, practical time to learn it through meditation only. But if you are getting knocked down by illusory punches over and over, you learn it pretty quickly, neh? Speaking in terms of ordinary, practical time, naturally. And it happens even faster with the swords. Anyway, that's why the Senkyo Sect practices martial arts. The only reason.

He gathers his legs under him, stands. It is time for us to go.

In ordinary, practical time, Kansen says with a chuckle.

Sendo harrumphs, brushes dirt from his robe. Wise guy, he says in English.

The sun is low now, and the afternoon is quiet, still. They

return to the door in the gate and go in. The monks from the karate class are just lining up to ring the evening bell, so they walk toward the main temple.

Sendo-gobosan, whose mat is to the left of his, stops before his mat and turns to face the altar. Kansen does the same. They then arrange themselves on their mats and sit in silence until all the others have done the same. The abbot enters, sits, lights incense and after a pause, begins the Heart Sutra. When that is over all fall into meditation. The clap of the wooden blocks at the end is shocking as always. Then they rise and walk a full circuit of the aisles. When all of the monks have returned to their spots in front of their respective mats, all bow, then file out to line up for the toilets. Once clear of the hall, hands go to the skirts of the robes, and the pace picks up almost to a run. All piss or try to piss in the long latrine. One or two go to the row of holes and squat. They return to the hall as individuals or in small groups, and much slower than the trip the other way. There are some whispers, but not many and none when back in the hall.

The sun has set during meditation, but a bit of twilight lingers. Still, the candlelight in the hall seems bright. The monks make up their beds without speaking, turn and bow toward the altar, go to bed, one by one. Sendo-gobosan and Kansen are among the earliest. Kansen listens to the later ones for a good half a minute before he is gone into a deep, dreamless sleep.

Sendo-gobosan awakens him in half-darkness. A single candle burns at the altar forty feet away. They make up their beds, hustle to the toilets and then to the well, a few older monks ahead of them, some younger ones sleepily behind. They return to the hall refreshed by the cold water, sit and prepare themselves for meditation. A few latecomers are still finding their way in when the bell begins to sound, but all are in place before it is finished.

After chanting and meditation Kansen is put to sweeping the walkways. Sendo-gobosan shows him where to find his thatch broom, where to start; apparently where to finish is up to him. Kansen watches him walk smartly away, his wooden sandals clacking on the stones.

He pays attention to the colors and patterns of the stones comprising the walkways, listens intently to birdsong and the soft wind in the trees. His morning is a joy. He sweeps and sweeps, breathing and listening and feeling the mist as it burns away, the sun when it comes, the slight breeze. The cedar scent of his sweat-moistened wooden sandals rises when the breeze drops. Now, now, all is now. Beyond, beyond, beyond Beyond. A pleasure beyond pleasure, a peace beyond peace, any peace he has ever known, even in meditation. He sweeps. What joy!

The midday bell. Brief meditation, We receive from above us. Brown rice, seaweed soup, pickles, tea. Delicious! A dear friend beside him. Grateful for these gifts. Indeed! The toilet. Squatting. Delightful!

The next few weeks go according to routine, up before light, chanting and meditation, sweeping, sutras, midday meal, floor polishing, sword and karate, evening chanting and meditation, sleep. He feels himself to be on the verge of an understanding unlike any he's had so far, the connections hover just outside of his consciousness all the time he is sweeping the damp walkways, are almost there when the bell sounds for sutra writing. He sighs, finding himself reluctant to stop sweeping, without any anticipatory interest in the sutra. Still, he turns on his wooden sandals and goes to put up his broom.

Sendo is waiting for him in the shed by the broom racks. His expression is grave. You are wanted in the abbot's quarters, he says.

Kansen wants to ask if he knows why, but just says, Yes, Gobosan.

He bows and racks his broom. Sendo has already turned his back and is walking away.

He follows the walkways across the open space wondering what this might be about, realizes it must have to do with Terayama—Reikyo-hoshi now, remember—and hopes the old man is not ill, that he has received no bad reports of Kansen's behavior as a monk. He shrugs inwardly. I've behaved like all the other monks. Just wait and see.

At the entrance to the abbot's quarters he kneels, calls out, I commit a discourtesy, hides his face on the boards. In a moment the door slides open.

Step up, says the abbot.

He raises his head and stands and bows and says Thank you. Inside, the abbot leads him to his private room. Tells him to sit in formal position and sits facing him.

Reikyo-hoshi has asked for you. He will explain some things to you and give you special instructions.

Yes, Soincho.

Do not be surprised by his appearance. It is in the nature of his practice.

Yes, Soincho.

The abbot looks at him intently, silent for some moments, as if he is considering saying something more. Finally he looks down at his desk, exhales with a long hiss.

All right. He is in the same room. Go now.

Yes, Soincho.

Kansen rises and bows and turns down the hall to the room he and Terayama—Reikyo-hoshi now, remember—had shared. He reaches the door and kneels and whispers, I commit a discourtesy, and waits. A slow, drawn-out reply comes at last, a voice he does not know. He slowly slides open the paper door.

Despite the abbot's warning he is shocked. He recognizes Terayama, but only just. The man has shrunk to barely half his size. His brown robe hangs around him and puddles voluminously on the tatami mat. He sits in the Lotus position with two bowls to his right. The skin of hands and face and feet and the little bit of exposed chest have gone to a deep brown, darker than any amount of sun could have made it. His eyes are downcast, though he makes a brief effort to raise them, and to make a small, fleeting smile.

Kansen-gobosan, he says, very slowly, in drawn out tones barely above a whisper.

Yes, Hoshi.

Come in. I have much to tell you.

Kansen knee-walks into the room, slides the door closed behind him. When he is in place facing Terayama he bows from his kneeling position.

Now, a real monk are you? he asks. New things you are learning?

Yes, Hoshi.

Well, now time for new lessons.

He raises a parchment hand to his shoulder, a characteristic gesture Kansen had not noticed before but now remembers. When he does a sweetness wafts from the old man's body, of pine, perhaps, or of a flower unknown to him.

Hanako-san, did she tell you about the Living Buddhas of the Senkyo Sect?

Yes, Hoshi.

Well, that is what I am doing. I am making a Living Buddha. I will try to explain.

He folds his hands in his lap, the movement again filling the air in the room with the strangely sweet smell.

The origin of this process begins in Tibet. It is called the 'Great Perfection,' and was still done there when the Chinese army went in a few years ago. But the intent is not exactly the same. The old ones actually made themselves disappear entirely, or left behind only some hair and fingernails for their disciples. Some of the greatest ones left only a small pile of jewels. For them, making a Living Buddha is a minor thing, a lesser thing to do. I am sure that for the students witnessing this it is a very great thing indeed. Since one who makes a Living Buddha helps many sentient beings, inspiring them over centuries, perhaps it is not really such a minor thing.

Hanako explained to you the doctrine of Becoming a Buddha in this Living Body, neh?

Yes, Hoshi.

She explained about the diet.

Yes, Hoshi.

Well, some Living Buddhas took the foods for as long as three thousand days. Kukai and some others, only one thousand. I have been taking them for one thousand, six hundred and forty days so far, but I have been active most of that time, teaching, and frankly, I have cheated a bit, as I was becoming weakened too quickly to continue my teaching. The abbot said it is all right, though, that all the movement helped spread the foods through my body more evenly than most, and that the sword and karate are also forms of meditation.

The old Chinese Taoists also sometimes did this, too. Actually, it may be from them that Kukai learned how it is done, when he went to China, where he learned the correct things to eat. Our Senkyo learned this from the thirteenth disciple of a disciple of Kukai, named Honmyo-kai, who himself became a Living Buddha at Senninzawa.

But there is another factor you must understand. We in Japan cannot make Living Buddhas without help. This is because, as you can see, even on our highest mountains the air is filled with moisture, with rain and snow all year long. So the diet alone is not enough to ensure completion. I have chosen you to be the one who will help me.

The old man's voice is fading to the merest whisper. He stops and raises one of the bowls at his side, sips from it, returns it to the mat, each movement excruciatingly slow and cautious. Kansen sits and watches this in great detail. He is not yet even ready to try to assimilate what he has just been told. He cannot speak, cannot even think. He watches Terayama's movements, listens to the rustle of his robe, the sipping of the liquid, the faint scratching as the cup is returned to the straw of the tatami mat. Within himself he can hear only the question, Why has he chosen me?

I have trained you for this very hard and very quickly, Kansen-gobosan. You have studied well and learned much. Now you must learn more.

Yes, Hoshi. He hears his voice as a frog-like croak.

You must learn which trees produce the correct nuts for my continued diet. You must learn the tree that produces the sap for my tea.

Yes, Hoshi.

My legs are almost dead already. Soon I will no longer be able to go to the toilet or clean myself. There is very little waste, but you will have to help me with these things. I do not know how long it will take, but a time will come when you will have to carry me up to that cave I showed you and seat me in it. During this time I will be in deep samadhi and will not be able to speak to you. You will have to close the door and stay there outside for some days, opening the door often to listen for my breathing. When I am no longer breathing you will have to burn charcoal in a brazier in the cave, with herbs and incense, which I have here in my kit. You must tend the fire with the charcoal and incense until the Living Buddha is completely dry, then seal the cave perfectly against all air.

He turns his head and eyes at that point, looking deeply into the blue of Kansen's. They register no sadness, only a calm intensity, a pure teacher's gaze.

Sendo-gobosan will teach you about the trees. He will give you the material to seal the cave and will not ask why you want it. Everything else you will have to do alone and in secret. Do you understand?

Yes, Hoshi, I understand.

Good.

From his bag he withdraws a few nuts and a vial with something brown in it. He hands them to Kansen and says, Show these to Sendo-gobosan. These are samples of what I will eat. He will know where to find them.

Yes, Hoshi.

Good. Now, Kansen-gobosan, you must understand that I am no longer Terayama. From this moment, I am only Reikyo, and will be only Reikyo until I become Reikyo-kai.

Kansen is suddenly pierced with sadness. He cannot contain himself.

Hoshi, I don't want you to die.

I will not die. You'll see. Reikyo-kai will be teaching for ten thousand years. Do not grieve. Do not even remember.

It is hard, but he manages to say Yes, Hoshi.

Leave me now. I will send for you when I need you.

Yes, Hoshi.

That is all, he says, closing his eyes and faintly adjusting his posture.

Yes, Hoshi.

Kansen rises and bows. Reikyo-hoshi has fallen into samadhi and does not acknowledge him.

Kansen stumbles outdoors stunned and confused by so many emotions his mind is frozen. He stares at the flagstones of the walkway, sees that they are littered with sand and vagrant leaves. He thinks, I must have missed this section. But then he comes to a crossing and has to look up to see which way to go. He thinks, I don't know which way to go. Where should I go?

He looks around the open quadrangle, sees the buildings, the sheds, the shrubs, the gravel and sand and flagstones and feels a fitful, nervous wind. Then he looks to his left at a reach of walkway he is sure he had swept in the morning and it too is littered and he realizes that it is because of this wind. He looks to the sky and sees patches of thick clouds racing past the sun and feels the air change back and forth from hot to cool as the light beneath the clouds changes from bright to shaded. Not knowing where to go or why to go anywhere he turns left and follows the flagstones toward the shed where his broom is racked and even knowing that to sweep in this wind is futile he has an irresistible urge to sweep, to clear the walkways, all will be clear if he can tread on clean flagstones, then he will know where to go.

He walks to the open shed and steps up onto the rough wood decking and takes his broom from the rack and begins to sweep the rough wood, even it is littered with sand and vagrant leaves, his eyes focus entirely on the rough wood as he sweeps his way toward the flagstones until he sees a pair of bare feet in wooden sandals in his path. He stops but does not look up. He just waits for them to go away.

Kansen-gobosan, a voice says.

He does not answer.

Kansen-gobosan, look up.

He blinks, a few rapid flutters, realizes that his eyes are gritty. Finally he raises his head with his eyes still closed and then opens them with much difficulty. He already knows that the feet in the wooden sandals will be Sendo's.

Yes, Gobosan, he says.

Put away your broom, Sendo says. It is almost time for the meal.

He shakes his head. I cannot eat, he says.

That's all right. But you must meditate.

He shakes his head again. I must think.

No. You must meditate.

Just then he hears the first boom of the great bell. He shakes his head yet again and wipes grit from his eyes and by the second stroke of the bell he has turned and walked to the rack and by the third he has racked his broom and listens to the most beautiful sound he has ever heard, the great bell, different today, no echoes but a wavering lingering melody as the wind takes the sound and plays with it, moves it around the sky and the mountains. He looks into Sendo's eyes and feels a small and rueful smile forming on his face because of the beauty of the bell and says, Yes, Gobosan.

They go to the main hall and find their mats and chant the sutra before the meal and then the silence falls and he goes where that takes him and when the food is served he finds he can eat a little.

After the meal and the chanting of the Thankful Sutra and the walking meditation Sendo gestures that Kansen is to follow.

They go to the consultation room behind the altar and then kneel and sit on their heels facing the sliding door of the back wall. Sendo slides open the door and they bow from their seats to Senkyo-kai. They sit then and contemplate the Living Buddha. The figure seems to contemplate them in return. The torn mouth suggests a smile, a kind of blessing.

After a time Sendo says, Stay here and think, if you need to think. Consult Senkyo-kai if you have any questions. He rises and bows and withdraws, leaving Kansen alone with the mummy. Kansen hears the door to the consultation room slide closed.

Gazing into the dead and desiccated face he begins to sort out the tumult of emotions he has just experienced. First is the sadness. His friend and teacher and mentor is dying, will soon be in the same condition as the corpse in front of him. The sadness of that is inescapable. He remembers their first meeting, the smiles they shared at seeing the shrine's moat and arch from the window of his apartment. The delight of their silent bicycle tour, the old man in his ball cap and track suit and sneakers. The huge fun of writing Rihaku's drinking poem with big brushes. The hours of private instruction at the dojo in Zentsuji. None of that ever again. No one else like his Terayama-sensei in his life before, nor will there be after. No one in the world. He squeezes his eyes shut, fights tears. Then he looks up again at the dead thing in front of him and finds its very existence macabre. What Terayama is doing, macabre.

You led him to this, you mummy, you corpse, you *thing*. What were you thinking?

There is no I, it says. There never was.

Is that what you believe? Believed?

No need to believe anything. Just see.

See what?

The mummy doesn't answer, just sits grinning at him, the torn smile a message he cannot read. He sits a little longer, looking into that face.

He bows, slides the door closed, stands and bows again. When he leaves the temple the wind has faded, the clouds have passed. He is blinded for a moment, has to pause under the shade of the eaves. He disappears into the magenta flash behind his eyes, stands completely still. He hears a gentle sound close to his ear, feels a brush of air on his cheek, smells a powdery warmth there. He opens his eyes and as he does a swallow flies from his shoulder and in this instant he knows what Senkyo-kai was smiling about.

No need to believe anything. Just see.

And hear and smell and taste and feel. What is here. Only what is here. Now.

This. Just see *this*.

And seeing *this*, he is freed from fear.

Light, almost afloat, he goes to find Sendo-gobosan. He has forgotten to give him the nuts and the vial. When Sendo sees him he suppresses a smile, takes a square of cloth from the sleeve of his robe and wipes West's shoulder, examines the gray stain on the cotton.

San Francisco, he says.

It takes West a second, but then he understands that Sendo means the saint, not the city.

し

The next morning after chanting and meditation Sendo signals him to follow. They go in the cool early dark to the dojo, where Sendo lights a candle and they change into black karate uniforms. They go then to a spot behind the toolshed, where Sendo rummages briefly with his back to Kansen, comes up with his pair of split-toed boots and his own rope sandals. They sit on the edge of the platform in front of the toolshed and change from their wooden sandals into this rougher footwear. When they are re-shod Sendo leads him to the front gate. Kansen sees he has added a small pack hung from a staff.

They don't follow the rutted road but turn to follow the eastern wall to the gate leading to the abbot's garden. There they turn east toward the grove where they'd first met. Sendo sets a quick pace despite the darkness. When they reach the stream bed it is completely dry. It is well into July now, and has rained very little over the last week or two.

We are going to the cave with the door, Sendo says. Do you know the way in the dark?

Kansen thinks he does, says Yes, Gobosan.

Sendo signals him to take the lead. He senses the path, though it has grown over considerably since early June. They climb gradually now, encountering the first stunted pines. Soon they are up into the forest, the trees taller, the ambient light of a starry sky blanked by their shadows. Kansen can no longer see anything of the path.

I've lost it, Gobosan, he says.

Sendo grunts and resumes the lead. Remember this tree, he says, and then look for that little space to the right.

Yes, Gobosan.

Kansen follows him toward that space. He feels that they are making too much to the south when Sendo says, Here. Remember this rock. Turn left exactly uphill when you reach it.

Yes, Gobosan.

He makes the turn uphill, and sees the shape of the great cedar blackening the sky.

Yes, Gobosan. The great cedar, right?

Right. Take the lead again.

They go straight to the great cedar, no trouble with that, but because of the new growth it takes Kansen a few tries to find the tiny break in the underbrush leading to the clearing. He does, finally, and once there can stride directly to where the door is hidden in the crevasse.

Good, Kansen-gobosan, Sendo says. Next time you lead all the way.

They sit then in the cool grass of the clearing. Sendo opens his pack and takes out his tiny brazier and teapot and a fistful of charcoal and starts a small fire. The eastern sky has paled slightly. The silence between them is comfortable as they wait for the charcoal to heat and the kettle to boil. By the time the tea is steeping the sky is pink in the east and the grasses have gone from black to light gray. A breeze stirs a rustling in the surrounding branches and a sparrow flits down from the cedar into the brush. They hear the screech of a hawk from deep in the forest.

I grew up in the forest not far from here, Sendo says as they sip the pungent buckwheat tea. My father was an educated man of Samurai family, but fortune turned against him in the time of the Mongolian war. He became nothing but a laborer, leaving my mother and me to live as we could. We had a hut in the mountains not far from here. When I was a child I spent all my days helping her to gather nuts and mushrooms and such in the woods. Until word came that my father had died and she sent me here to Senkyo Temple. Ever since then I have been a monk.

However, before that she found a grove with several lacquer trees in it, and learned to draw the sap and could sell that each autumn to the lacquerware artists in the city. That sap was what was in the vial Reikyo-hoshi gave you. It can also be used in small quantities for a special sort of tea. Because it is now owned by a large company, we cannot go to the grove my mother found. Although it is too early for the sap, there are some lacquer trees in this area too. I will show you and teach you to draw the sap. Little will be needed.

Sendo slurps the last of his tea and sets about packing his tea implements. The sun is fully up now in a clear sky, the light slanting golden through the array of forest greens. He rises, stretches. Kansen does the same. Sendo hands him a cloth bag from his pack. Then they are off.

But first, there is a particular pine, Sendo says as they walk uphill to the north. It is the one that gives us the light-colored nuts. And then, the chestnuts. It is far too early for them, but I will show you for later.

The next several hours are among the happiest Kansen has ever known. He is fascinated by Sendo's lessons, the different colors and textures of barks, the particular smells and arrangements of needles and leaves, the exact way the cone of the Kaya pine must be split open to reveal the edible nut within, the precise angle to make the cut in the Urushi bark to draw the sap. The majesty of the great Kuri chestnut trees, the patterns of last year's nuts on the ground where they have fallen or been stripped by squirrels. This is a world of wonders he has seen before but never quite seen, the subtext of a poem he'd read but never understood until it was parsed for him. He wanders in awe and joy.

The sun is quartering into the west when their packs are nearly bursting with their collected pine cones. Sendo has him lead the way back to the great cedar, and then back down the morning's path. He is able to do this unerringly. When they have reached the temple's gate and crossed the grounds to the kitchens and have emptied their sacks to the pleasure of the cooks there, Kansen bows deeply to Sendo.

Thank you, Sendo-gobosan. It has been a wonderful day.

Sendo grunts and bows perfunctorily. But Kansen thinks he sees the smallest hint of a smile in the corner of the older man's mouth.

They make two more trips into the forest to gather pine cones, Kansen leading and finding the cave and spotting the various trees without difficulty both times. On the second of these outings they set small taps in one of the lacquer trees.

Late in July Sendo declares them ready for the sap to be drawn. It is a little soon, he says, but we will not need much, I think. Kansen doesn't ask him why that might be.

It must be early in August when they go to the lacquer tree. They open the taps and fill the vials with sap and Sendo then takes a small box lined with silk and stuffed with paper and packs the vials carefully in it. When they return Sendo tells him to take the box to the abbot. A young monk meets him at the doorway and accepts the box formally.

A week or so later he is called to the abbot's quarters to see Terayama.

Reikyo-hoshi needs you now, the abbot says.

He finds his teacher prostrated before the little room's shrine. His spindly legs are locked in the Lotus position, his feet exposed and almost black, his heels pointed toward the ceiling. His knees and elbows rest on an old blanket, which is fouled with a few spatters of dark feces. There is still the sweet woodsy scent, but it is now mixed with the stench of wastes. It is clear what he must do.

He fetches a bucket of warm water and some rags from the baths and hurries back to the room. Terayama has not moved. Kansen touches his shoulder gently, tells him that he will now clean him. Then cleans him. Then carefully lifts him and removes the fouled blanket. As he folds it he sees that it is printed in one corner, Imperial Japan Armed Forces. He places it on the wooden floor just outside the sliding doors.

He knows he must find a replacement, searches the closet at the back of the room and finds a stack of them, Imperial Japan Armed Forces. On top of the pile is a note scrawled with a small brush, which he puts aside unread. He smells the blankets, they are freshly laundered, he opens the top one to a quarter of its full size, places it on the mat behind Terayama.

Will you sit now, Hoshi? he asks.

He thinks he sees a nod, or at least knows he feels acquiescence, and so carefully and gently he raises Terayama to a sitting position facing the door. The body weighs nothing. The face is composed, a parchment mask. He kneels and leans close to the face and feels the least subtle passage of air through its nose and mouth. He arranges the brown robe to fall neatly and then sits formally facing this man, Reikyo-hoshi, once Terayama-sensei, his teacher and friend. He quietly chants the final mantra of the Heart Sutra,

Gyate, gyate, hara gyate, hara so gyate.

Beyond, beyond, even beyond Beyond goeth the priest.

He rises and goes to tidy the closet, sees the scrawled note, its characters ill-formed, its vertical lines scattered like grasses. Reads it.

I can no longer speak. I can no longer eat. I will take the lacquer tree tea twice each day. When there is only the last sliver of this August moon, carry me up to the cave. You know what to do after that.

Reikyo

He returns to sit with Reikyo. In a short time a small gesture of the withered hand indicates that he wants to sit facing the shrine. Kansen rises and gently turns him. Then another small gesture suggests that he should leave. He bows and withdraws.

That night as he returns to the main hall from the toilets he notes that the moon is in its last quarter. Soon, then. It will be soon.

He goes twice each day to visit Terayama Reikyo-hoshi, cleans him, gives him a fresh blanket to sit on, serves him the lacquer tree tea, one small sip at a time. Each night he sees that the moon slowly thins. He knows that none of this can be reversed any more than can the moon be sped or slowed. His heart is breaking.

Then the night comes when the moon rises sickle-thin, and he must, he knows tonight he must. He goes from the toilets to the dojo and dons his black karate uniform and at the vestibule picks up his split-toed boots and goes to the room in the abbot's quarters and lifts Reikyo-hoshi, blanket and all, and carries him down the hall to the doors, seats him on the platform while he fastens his boots, then carries him to the garden and through the garden to the low gate in the wall and down through the grove through the stream bed, still dry, and up into the forest, this tree, the little space to the right, this rock, then straight uphill to the great cedar. Through the break in the underbrush and across the clearing. He seats Terayama Reikyo-hoshi on his blanket on the dry grass and goes to the cave and opens the wooden door and then picks up Terayama Reikyo-hoshi and seats him on the wooden platform there and smells the must of cave, dry now too, and kneels before his former teacher and chants again,

Beyond, beyond, even beyond Beyond, goeth the priest.

Then he slowly and very gently closes the door and kneels before it and finds that his eyes and cheeks are wet.

He rises and arranges the blanket so that he can sit on a corner of it with his back to the door so as to guard it. He sits then in half-Lotus and pulls the rest of the blanket around his shoulders and draws the last corner of it over his shaven head, the very picture, he thinks, of Bodhidharma himself. He chants the Heart Sutra under his breath and even finishes the final mantra without choking and soon falls into the deep trance of samadhi. When this peaceful emptiness leaves him he opens his eyes to shades of orange glowing among the branches of the great cedar and knows he has been hours and hours away in the emptiness.

Straightening his legs is an exquisite agony. Slowly, slowly. He cannot feel his feet at all. He lies back on the ground and waits. When his feet begin to hurt as much as his knees and hips he rolls over to lie face down and then forces himself into the Dog and then the Cobra poses, back and forth, until he can actually move his feet and his knees and hips no longer burn. He feels refreshed and limber and strong and young, and then remembers his duty.

The door creaks as it opens, particles of dusty earth fall from its ancient wood. Behind it he sees that Terayama sits exactly as he'd been left in the night, a presence almost surprising to

Kansen. Was he expecting the Resurrection? He leans in, puts his ear to the mouth and nose. Yes, there still is breath. He tidies the teacher's robe where it had draped awry when he'd seated him in the darkness of the night before. He wants to speak, say Good Morning, something, but knows he must not. He closes the door carefully and then looks out over the brightening forest and wonders what to do.

He has brought neither water nor food. Dare he go to the little spring just up the hill? Dare he drink from it if he did? Can he go to the Kaya pine and gather some cones to eat?

He decides that he cannot. He must guard the cave and its precious contents. His duty.

So he practices his dozen or so karate kata until the sun actually tops the peaks to the east, then kneels and sits on his heels and does not meditate but watches the sparrows flit from branch to branch of the great cedar and drop into the shrubs below, which now have only a smattering of tiny red berries left, and into the grasses of the clearing, which now have sprigs bearing thousands of tiny seeds. These birds chatter rather than sing, though he hears birdsong from somewhere in the forest, wrens, perhaps, or finches. Sendo has not taught him about birds, but he knows this about them, that their consciousness, as well as his own, is constantly in the process of creating the world.

He meditates for a while, then rises and meditates walking, a nearly circular route around the edges of the clearing. Three times around. During the third circuit he loses the mind of meditation and finds himself searching the grasses and the shrubs for something he might eat. Dare he try the berries? Clearly not. The grass seeds? Probably not. He ends this third circuit before the door, stops and opens it and again puts his ear to his teacher's nose and mouth and again feels the faint movement of air.

And so the rest of his day goes, these practices repeated over hours and hours. The only change is in that now, when he empties his mind in meditation, the sense of emptiness in his belly disappears. And if it sometimes returns, he chants all the sutras he can remember, drawing the sound from deep in his lower abdomen until it feels filled with sound down there. He watches the sunset, listening to the last frantic searches of the sparrows, their rustling in the needles of the cedar as at twilight they maneuver for their night perches. It takes a long time for the sky to go to stars. He returns to the cave and feels the breath of his teacher and then closes the door and arranges the blanket and curls himself into a ball and sleeps.

Sometime in the night Kappa comes to him. He wakes or dreams that he wakes and sits formally facing the silhouette of his frog-like familiar.

Good evening, Kappa-san, he says. Why have you come?

Kappa does not speak, but from the direction of the spring uphill comes the croak of a frog. It says, Because you need help.

Thank you, Kansen says, but I will be all right.

Neither Kappa nor the distant frog say anything. The starlight now seems brighter, Kansen can make out the features of Kappa's face. He has seen it before, in a dream and at the pond near Imabara and cast into the sword guard Hanako once gave him long ago. They look into each other's eyes for a considerable time, or so it seems to Kansen.

I can help you, the frog croaks at last, or perhaps this time it actually is the Kappa.

How can you help me?

I will guard the cave while you go to the spring for water and find some cones from the Kaya pine.

I cannot let you do that. It is my duty.

They sit silently again. A whisper of a breeze causes the cedar to sigh. A cloud obscures the stars for a few moments, then moves away. Another follows it. Kansen lies back down and pulls the blanket around him.

I can go to the pond and bring you water, says Kappa, shocking Kansen out of sleep. And I can gather some of the cones and bring them, too.

Kansen considers this offer. How can you bring me water? he asks.

There is a bowl shaped into the top of my skull. I can bring it in that.

Another cloud passes beneath the starlight. Another waft of wind follows it, this one chilling. Kansen sleeps a little, and wakes to the discomfort of dew on the blanket. He sees that there are no more stars. He bites a corner of the blanket and sucks the dew from it.

Thank you, Kappa-san, he mutters.

The next time he wakes it is in the heavy sky of a gray dawn. The wild wind whips the cedar into a noisy frenzy and blows branches and leaves across the clearing. Kansen huddles in his damp blanket and shivers. Then he gets up and washes his face with the wettest corner of the blanket and sits and chants the Heart Sutra through and then again until he has warmed from within. He rises and stretches, the Dog and the Cobra, and then goes to the cave and again feels his teacher's breath and then meditates in half-Lotus and then walks again the perimeter of the clearing in deep samadhi and after the third circuit becomes aware of the wind and the detritus it has blown into the grasses and finds among the branches and needles a few cones of the Kaya pine.

Thank you, Kappa-san.

He gathers them and sits again by the door of the cave and sets himself to opening them, hard to do without a knife but there is a shard of rock sharp enough. He eats, and then it begins to rain.

He strips and bathes cold in the rain and then huddles in his drenched blanket throughout the day, meditating sometimes, sleeping sometimes, refusing every daydream and dreaming sometimes but only in shallow, disconnected images. Whenever the rain takes a pause he looks in on his teacher. Still breathing.

Night comes quickly and the rain stops and the wind does too. The sparrows have not left the branches of the cedar all the day. He wrings out the blanket and his karate uniform and looses the flaps of his soaked cloth split-toed boots and dresses again and eats the last of his Kaya pine nuts and after checking on his teacher one more time—still breathing—he curls into the wet clothes and shivers. He is not sure if he has slept when he senses the presence of Kappa where he had last seen it.

Thank you for the nuts and water, Kappa-san, he says.

Kappa folds its webbed hands and lowers its eyes but does not speak.

Kansen sleeps again and wakes to find a fox curled into his body, warming his belly, her head resting in the crook of his elbow and her breath—warm, so warm—fanning his face. He looks down and sees her face, the moist black of her nose, the fine white whiskers on her snout fluttering slightly, her eyes closed, as peaceful in his warmth as he is peaceful in hers.

He glances beyond and sees the Kappa sitting quietly nearby and smiles at it.

He sleeps. Oh, how he sleeps. When he wakes it is to bright sunlight streaming from the eastern peaks into the glistening branches of the cedar and onto the diamond-studded grass. Close to the ground, fog clings to the shrubs. Steam rises from his sun-cooked blanket. Kappa and the fox have gone. He stretches and sits and washes his face with the soggy blanket and chants the Heart Sutra and goes to the cave and puts his ear to his teacher's mouth and nose and this time there is no breath. He draws back, stunned, wondering if he is not quite awake enough, then leans in again and listens for a long time but there is still no breath and there will never be any more breath ever again.

Beyond, beyond hath gone the priest.
Oh Sensei, goodbye, goodbye.

ひ

He feels uncertain as to the next step to take. He must go back
down to the temple and find Terayama's kit so that he can make a
fire from the charcoal and incense in it. But he must also guard the
cave, allow nothing to disturb the body within. He thinks. No
human is likely to stumble onto the place, but just in case he must
camouflage the door, make it invisible. Then, animals. That will be
fairly easy, just stuff the blanket in the obvious gaps, secure it
there with rocks. Yes, he can do all that.

So he sets himself to it, stuffing the blanket and collecting
rocks from the sides of the boulders to secure it, then gathering
the wind-blown leaves and branches left by the storm. The great
cedar has lost several living branches. He arranges them artfully
over the door so that look as hard as he might he cannot see it
from any angle. It will do.

This takes him most of the morning, and he is very hungry
and thirsty after the work. Even though he knows he will be too
late for the meal, he sees no choice but to go down to the temple
right away. The fires must dry the Living Buddha soon, right now,
or it will rot where it sits.

He will, not *it* will.

So he tidies up all signs he can of his having spent three
nights in the clearing and goes to the small opening in the

underbrush and when he emerges from it he sees Sendo-gobosan sitting quietly under a bent old pine tree, Terayama's kit and one of his own beside him.

Good morning, Kansen-gobosan, he says. Perhaps you are hungry?

Kansen says Good morning and goes to sit next to Sendo under the bent pine. Sendo takes a box out of his kit and a water flask. As he is preparing their cold meal Kansen asks him if that is Reikyo-kai's kit, though he is sure he recognizes it.

It is Reikyo-hoshi's kit, not that of Reikyo-kai, Sendo says. I know of no Reikyo-kai. He asked me to leave it with you.

Forgive me. Of course. The kit of Reikyo-hoshi. Thank you.

They chant the brief Sutra before the meal and then eat, not talking. Kansen has some difficulty using his chopsticks, wanting to gobble the brown rice and vegetables like a pig. But he manages to eat slowly and to sip water from the flask rather than to guzzle it. When they have finished Sendo produces two small white cloths and two slices of Takuan pickle, with which they clean their boxes and then eat the pickles and fold the cloths. Sendo packs all that away in his kit, pours all of the water into one flask and places that next to Terayama's kit. He then takes out another box and places that there too. He then closes his kit and rises. Kansen rises too.

There are two buckets behind this tree and some tools. I will leave them here for now. Put them back there when you return to the temple.

Yes, Gobosan.

I will leave you now. I have not seen you.

I understand.

Sayonara.

They bow. Sendo disappears quickly into the forest. Kansen waits a few minutes, then goes behind the tree and finds the buckets. They are of wood and are covered with wooden lids and on one of the lids is some folded cloth and two different kinds of trowel. He puts these aside and lifts the lid. One bucket is full to the brim with a dry gray powder, the other with water. Kansen knows he is to mix the cement for sealing the door to the cave.

He replaces the lid and the cloth and the trowels, then goes to Terayama's kit. He kneels before it, unties the corners and looks in. There is a small box of wooden matches secured by the knot. On top of what he knows will be charcoal and incense there is a piece of paper with writing on it. He unfolds it and opens it. The handwriting is strong and clear, it had to have been written before Terayama had weakened. He reads.

Kansen-gobosan,

This is exactly enough charcoal and exactly enough incense to complete the making of the Living Buddha. If I am wrong and it is not exactly enough, the failure will be mine and not yours. Be sure there is enough air in the cave to keep the fire burning until all of the charcoal and incense are burned to nothing. Then let the smoke clear out of the cave and seal the door with the wattling. Seal it perfectly, so that no air can enter.

I don't know if you will be at the cave when it is opened in three years and the Living Buddha is removed to the temple and dressed in his red robes and golden cowl. But know that it will be done, and that when it is done you will have made it possible. All monks of the Senkyo Sect *will be grateful to Kansen-gobosan for ten-thousand years.*

Reikyo

Kansen folds the letter and touches it to his forehead and tucks it into his jacket. What a thing to be able to do. What courage. What suffering and fear have to be overcome. All monks willingly give up the things of the world to live on rice and pickles and seaweed. Senkyo and Hommyo and now Reikyo have given up even those things. For what?

To see. *This.*

The whole history of the sect flows through him. He remembers the dream image of the row of mummies in the cave. Such men, over centuries and centuries.

He sits for a time, then re-ties the kit and carries it through the opening in the underbrush and to the door of the cave and ponders just how he will set this fire without burning the platform or the door or the Living Buddha within. He kneels and sits on his heels and looks at the door he has worked to camouflage so pointlessly.

First, clear the door. Then lay the fire. Then start the fire. Then almost-close the door. Feed the fire until all the fuel is gone. Then clear the smoke. Then use the cement to seal the door.

For three years.

He sighs, wonders how long it will take for all that charcoal and incense to burn itself out. More than a day, he is sure. He is grateful that Sendo has thought to leave him food and water. Then he rises and begins his sequence of tasks.

It is mid-afternoon before he can get the charcoal started, because he has only the paper of Terayama's note for kindling and he is unwilling to burn it. He has had to find dry patches of dead grass and small twigs which have not quite dried and some dead branches which he has had to strip of wet bark using one of the trowels, and then as this kindling burns he has to be careful that its flames don't reach the platform or Terayama's body. All that before he can start adding charcoal at all, and only the smallest fragments of that at first, so when it is finally all alight and he can add the incense and almost-close the door the sun is halfway into the west. It is clear that he will have to stay the night monitoring the fire, and will not be able to seal the door until morning at the earliest. At sunset he nibbles a little of his cold brown rice and sips a little of his water, shakes out his dirty blanket and sits in it again, like Bodhidharma. He meditates and periodically checks on the fire, adjusting the glowing coals with the trowel. Kappa does not come, nor does the fox. It seems a very long night.

At first light the fire still smolders, but barely. He opens the door fully to allow the fumes to clear, rakes the ashes and covers them with earth from under a rock near the door. Then closes the door as tightly as he can and begins to mix the cement and then to spread it into every crack and seam. It is noon when all the cement is gone from the bucket. He can see no more cracks or seams. He uses the last of his water to dampen the cloth Sendo has left him and cleans his hands as best he can with it. Then he camouflages the door one more time. He gathers the lunch box and the flask and Terayama's kit. On his way back to the temple he returns the buckets and cloth and trowels to their place behind the old bent pine.

As he follows the path downhill he sees a dusty cloud and hears the rumble of a diesel engine, and as he rounds a turn he sees the top of a truck on the rutted road below, heading for the temple. The semi-annual delivery of supplies, he assumes. He heads down toward the road, thinking it would be best to return openly through the front gate.

The one young monk guarding the gate bows coldly to him as he enters, and in an icy tone tells him to go to the abbot's quarters. Kansen thanks him and does so. He kneels before the door and knocks on the platform and calls out, I commit a discourtesy. The young monk who serves the abbot's quarters slides open the door a fraction, says Wait, very curtly. Kansen continues to kneel as minutes pass. Then the abbot slides the door open with a bang.

You, Kansen, he says (no gobosan). Look at you. You are filthy and unshaven and have been absent from meditation and working and classes for four days, out playing in the woods or drunk in the village or whatever you have been doing. You are finished here. You will return to Takamatsu in the truck.

All in the coarse voice you hear behind the subtitles in old samurai movies, and punctuated with his slamming the door shut. A moment later the young monk opens it again and throws Kansen's kit into the gravel beyond. The truck will come around to the front gate in a few minutes, he says coldly. Wait out on the road.

Kansen says nothing, rises, picks up his kit and goes back out through the gate, walks a few paces up the rutted road, drops his kit and crouches beside it. He understands why this has been done to him—it is to keep the secret of the Living Buddha from the other monks—but it hurts nevertheless.

And he will sorely miss his life at the monastery.

も

The driver is a taciturn little man in a peaked cap and blue jumpsuit wearing the same sort of split-toed cloth boots West wears. The truck is old and the cab is dirty and the ride down the rutted road is long and rough and dusty. The diesel fumes fill the space despite the open windows. The driver never speaks a word. The track leads them north and west of the forest he and Sendo have explored so thoroughly, into a landscape more of rocks than of trees. It leads eventually to a wider graveled stretch, and by late afternoon to a paved road. There is little traffic. West dozes until near sunset, when the road opens into a four-lane highway. Then the noise of passing traffic and soon the flash and glare of headlights wakes and then blinds him.

He can't be sure, but he thinks their route has taken him east of Takamatsu. This is confirmed when the truck slows and turns right and West recognizes the southern section of Chuo Avenue and sees that they are heading north on it, into town. The driver stops at the light at Hachiman Street and says, Here. Out. Hurry.

There are few lights, few cars, few people on foot or on bicycles. He passes a restaurant and a coffee house and realizes that he is very hungry but has no idea if he has any money at all. He hasn't needed any in a year and two months. Walking on pavement in his split-toed cloth boots is jarring, the air stinks of car and truck and the trains. He plods.

At the brightly-lit arch before the shrine he pauses to bow briefly, then, having the light, he digs into his kit and finds his wallet and the key to his apartment. He turns and walks to the building and climbs the three flights of exposed stairs and fumbles in the dark until he has the door unlocked, steps inside. Drops his pack. Sits in the dark vestibule to remove the boots from his aching feet.

Then he opens the door to the bath and snaps on the light, starts the water heater. Goes to the kitchen, puts on the light. It is clean. Perfectly. Nothing as he left it, but rather as he had found it when he'd first entered it with Terayama three years before. He finds some packaged noodles and a small bottle of sakê and heats the sakê and then the noodles and then eats and drinks. It's not much, but he hasn't had any sakê for a year and a half and it hits him hard. The water is hot by then and he showers, stumbles into the four-and a half-mat room and finds bedding in the closet and lays it out and lies down on it and is gone in a minute.

He wakes to the six strokes of the muffled morning bell, lies waiting for the sound of the eastbound morning JNR express. When it rattles over the trestle he gets up, showers again, puts on a sleeping robe. Finds tea in the kitchen and boils water for it. Then for the first time opens the door to the six mat room. The shrine is empty. No sword, no inkstone, nothing. The bookcase is not empty, but the karate and sword books Terayama had left for him and all his rolls of calligraphy are gone. He goes to the closet and finds one blue suit and one white shirt and one necktie and a pair of black loafers in a plastic bag. That is all there is of his in it. He is slow this morning and still tired and the message in all this is not clear to him immediately.

He steeps his tea and looks for something to eat with it but there is nothing. He goes to the bath and looks in the mirror. He has a quarter inch brush cut on his head and a beard of the same length. He sips tea as he shaves his face, arbitrarily picking a length for his sideburns. Then he checks his wallet. He is relieved to find a few hundred yen in it.

The passing of the train and the level of activity on the street below tell him that it is a weekday. Almost certainly he is expected at Yamazaki Industries. He dresses in his suit and tie and the pair of his loafers and goes down to the street and to the little restaurant where he'd had his first breakfast with Terayama and eats the set breakfast and feels ready to face what he knows will be a difficult day. This leaves him without enough money to take a cab to the office, so he goes around to the back of the apartment building to find his bicycle. It is gone too. So he takes the long walk to Marugame-machi, at a leisurely pace to save his clothes from the coming August heat. He passes the martial arts supply shop, just opening, and the corner of the wall of the Zen temple, where the bronze Amida Buddha peeks at him through the trees; the Pachinko parlor, where no one is yet playing, the shop of Buddhist religious articles, open but with no customers yet. Under the covered street it is cooler. His bicycle is in the lobby behind the staircase at Yamazaki entrance. He goes upstairs.

Miss Oka starts when he enters and covers her sudden intake of breath with a hand over her mouth. She stands frozen for a moment. He says Good Morning and she is unable to answer, just gives him a cursory bow. Mr. Ikeda looks up from his desk and says Good Morning, very quietly. Hirano stands and bows but says nothing. West goes to his desk. There is nothing on it or in any of the cubbyholes. He sits anyway and waits for something to happen.

Yamazaki-bucho arrives a little later, rumpled and dis-heveled as ever. He sees West at his desk and says, Come. West follows him into his office. It is as before, dusty and cluttered and the window is still dirty. Yamazaki stares out at it, his back to

West. West remains standing, waits.

Yamazaki heaves a sigh and without turning to face him, tells West, You are fired, of course.

I understand, West says.

You have been gone for over a year. Your visa has expired. There is no more work for you.

I understand.

Yamazaki turns then and without looking at West sits at his desk, picks up the phone and dials. There is an exchange in rapid Japanese which West can barely follow but guesses correctly is about airplane reservations. Yamazaki makes some notes, hangs up the phone.

You are booked from Takamatsu airport to Osaka International at eleven tomorrow morning. From there you will fly to San Francisco. My brother will meet you there. We have shipped all your things to him.

I see.

There is some money left in your account at the Hyakujushi Bank. Close the account today.

Yes, Bucho.

You may stay in the apartment tonight. Leave for the airport by taxi no later than nine o'clock in the morning.

Yes, Bucho.

That is all.

Yes, Bucho. Thank you. Sayonara.

Yamazaki waves a hand. West leaves the office, bows to Miss Oka and Mr. Ikeda and to Hirano and says Sayonara to each of them. None of them speaks, but each bows slightly, Miss Oka from where she stands near the tea table, Ikeda and Hirano from their desks.

He goes to the bank and closes his account and collects much more cash than he expected, several hundred thousand yen in large bills. It is barely noon when he leaves the bank and finds

Hirano waiting for him.

Join me for lunch, Hirano says.

They go to their usual restaurant, order, sit. Hirano has ordered one small flask of sakê with two cups. When it comes he pours for both of them.

So this is goodbye, he says. Kampai.

They drain the cups. Hirano fills them again. All this is because of the secret, he says.

I know.

You will probably never be able to come back to Takamatsu, and it will be a long time before you can come back to Japan at all.

I know.

Good.

The food comes and they eat it silently. It is too rich for West after two years of brown rice and seaweed. Fish and chicken, he can't eat much of it. When the meal is over Hirano insists on paying and says, You have learned much. You carry many secrets. Some of them maybe dangerous. Be careful and quiet back in America.

I will. Thank you, Kyoshin-gobosan.

Sayonara, Kansen-gobosan.

America. He can no longer even imagine it. He goes to a Kinokunya bookstore and buys three paperback novels, two in English and a Japanese translation of one of them. Must prepare for a long flight to that strange land he has all but forgotten.

せ

He sits at the kitchen table in his summer robe reading one of the paperbacks when he hears the key in the door. The last time he gave a thought to the time was when the bell rang its six strokes. That was hours and hours ago. It has to be she at the door.

He marks his page and stands, watching her in the vestibule through the mottled glass door as she places her shopping bag on the platform. As she straightens he slides open the door. Welcome, Hanako-san, he says. His voice is thick with its long silence and with the excitement of seeing her.

She does not smile or bow. Her hair hangs long and bangs fall almost into her eyes. She wears a clinging, almost transparent red dress that barely covers her pubis and a pair of red stilettos and clearly nothing else. She steps up to him and stands looking up into his eyes, her face just inches from his, waiting.

He pulls her to him and holds her to him and finds her mouth with his and it is soft and open and full of wet tongue. They exchange their breath until they are both gasping.

Now, she whispers. Right now.

He turns her so that the kitchen table supports her and he lifts the wispy bit of cloth she wears and opens his robe and enters her and is amazed by how all this feels, it is she, she is here, this is not the murky dream world of the last year, foxes and the Kappa and the caves this is here, she is here, this is now, she is now and forever. He explodes into her and nothing has ever been so real.

For a long time afterward he cannot move, he is entirely present but emptied, time has disappeared. Gradually he becomes aware of the glaring fluorescent light, the absurd formica of the table as a frame for her long black hair. He lifts her upright, still inside her, bends at the knee so that she can stand. They stay that way until he softens. Even after that they cling to one another.

Eventually he feels her withdrawing, not physically but he knows her mind has moved out of this time and has gone somewhere ahead. He loosens his grasp and she hers and still without a word, this time without even a glance, she pulls herself gently from him and steps around him and walks with loud clicks of her heels on the tile toward the bath. In a few moments he hears the hiss of the shower.

While she is gone he rinses his face and his crotch in the kitchen sink and then goes to the front room and makes up the bedding. He looks out the window and down at the moat and the shrine's arch and bridge. The night is still. He hears the haunting melody of the bamboo flute from somewhere down Hachiman Street and it strikes him in the heart. It will be the last time he'll ever hear it. America.

When she comes to him it is barefoot on tiptoe. She puts her arm around him and looks out with him. They stay like that for a long time and then he says, They've thrown me out.

I know, she says. After what you've done, they have no choice.

Don't you mean, We have no choice? You were all in it together.

She doesn't answer. He turns to her and she turns away. I've brought some whiskey, she says.

I don't want whiskey.

Yes you do. Just a little.

He continues to stare out the window as she goes to her bag in the vestibule and then to the kitchen. He finds he is trying to memorize the scene, the moat and the arch and the bridge, remembering Three-Five-Seven day, the children in their colorful kimono and straw sandals and the hovering parents in their subdued and elegant kimono trekking to the shrine for its god's blessings. The first blossoms of the plum trees in March. New Year's Eve and the hundred and eight strokes of the bell and the quiet crowds receiving their printed fortunes from the Shinto priestess. Never again. America.

She returns with the bottle and two glasses of whiskey and invites him to sit by sitting, next to the bedding, on the tatami mat. He does and she hands him a glass and without words offers hers for the clinking of glasses and they do that and then sip. The whiskey strikes his tongue sharply at first and then does what it is meant to do. The only light in the room is the glow in the window from the streetlights below. They hear the clank of shunting freight trains from far in the distance, the clatter of wooden sandals as someone crosses the bridge to ask the god for a cure for insomnia. They sip.

Because you are a foreigner, she says.

What has that got to do with it?

It has to do with your Special Assignment.

To kill Bankyo? The renegade monk in California?

No. Bankyo died years ago, as a soldier in Burma. Your Special Assignment was to help Terayama-sensei become the Living Buddha, Reikyo-kai.

This leaves him at a loss. He can make no sense of it. He has believed all along that he was being trained so that he would go back to America and see to the death of Bankyo, murderer, pornographer, betrayer of the Senkyo Sect during the war. He understands why a foreigner might be needed for that. But he cannot follow her thinking when she tells him that a foreigner was needed for the making of the Living Buddha.

I don't understand, he says. You will have to explain this.

She sighs heavily, drinks a considerable swallow of the whiskey. I know I do, she says. But I don't want to.

He waits. Her head is bowed. She stares into her glass as if there might be a way to disappear into it. He waits.

It goes back to the war, she says, still staring into the glass. To the destruction of the temple on Mount Koya and the burning of the Living Buddhas, Bankyo's betrayal.

She pauses, sips, looks back down into her glass.

Bankyo's original name was Yamazaki.

She looks to see that he has grasped the importance of this, then goes on.

The Yamazaki family were rich and dedicated to the temple. They were left in deep shame by what Bankyo did. They secretly financed the building of the temple in the Tosa mountains. When the war was over they continued to finance it and do still to this day. Out of a duty based on shame.

While this makes some things clear, it is still far from answering his question. He waits. Sips.

There has not been a Living Buddha since then, she continues. When Terayama-sensei realized he could make one in this living body, he told old Yamazaki-kaicho, you remember him from the banquet, the old man in kimono? Anyway, much had to be done to make it possible and safe.

You see, while it is not illegal in itself in Japan, it is considered a form of suicide. Suicide is not illegal in itself here, either. But assisting a suicide is illegal under all but a few circumstances, and none of them apply to the making of a Buddha in this living body.

Also, the only legal way to dispose of a dead body in Japan is to cremate it. Making a mummy, then, is not allowed under that law. So for these reasons it must be kept absolutely secret. Otherwise, if the authorities find out, the assistant will be put in jail and the Living Buddha will be burned.

That is how it reaches back to the war. The Senkyo Sect has had enough Living Buddhas burned and does not want that ever to happen again.

Now he understands all the secrecy. He understands why Terayama made sure he could not find his way back to Tosaguchi and the train station. It explains why the truck took such a complicated route back to Takamatsu.

How many people know? he asks.

Only five. You, I, Yamazaki-kaicho, the abbot at the temple, and Sendo-gobosan. No one else.

Not Hirano?

No. He knows there is something, but he does not know what it is.

He thinks about it some more, doesn't know yet how he feels about it, how he should feel about it. He frames another question, an obvious one.

That's all clear, he says. But why did they need a foreigner?

She seems to be finished, sips, still won't look at him, looks anywhere else. Shakes her head from side to side. Looks back down into her glass. Nothing she sees there seems to help her. He waits.

You leave tomorrow. You will go back to America and will never be allowed to come back to Japan, because you have let your visa expire. And even if you told anyone, they would not believe you. The Tosa Mummy Returns. The Making of a Modern Mummy. You would appear a fool. Such stories would never even reach Japan.

He slugs the rest of his whiskey in a gulp. Chokes, takes the burn. Used, he thinks, just used. To make an illegal corpse.

All my martial training?

It was to keep you focused. The year of training in Zentsuji where you were kept as a prisoner? That was hard on Terayama-sensei. He was ready to make the Living Buddha months before that. But they had to make you strong enough to do what you were needed to do. And they had to keep you until your visa ran out.

All this just to avoid a few legal problems which might well never have come up anyway.

Kansen-gobosan, she says, it was terribly important to the Senkyo Sect. You did a very brave and difficult thing, and you did it well. The few of us who know of it admire you for it and are grateful. Think. If you had been told that helping Terayama-sensei to make a Living Buddha was your Special Assignment, would you have studied so hard and learned so much? Would you even have considered doing it?

It takes him a while but he admits that he would not have, at least not in the early stages. He knows that it doesn't matter that he has been manipulated, because what he has learned can never be rendered worthless or absurd. The self-mastery they have shown him, all they have taught him. And in the end he has to admit to himself that he is relieved to know he doesn't have to kill someone back in the States. Only one thing still rankles.

And you? he asks. What was your part in all this?

She reaches across to him and at first he thinks she means to touch his hand but instead she takes his glass from him and pours more whiskey into it and returns it and then pours a little more into her own. Sips. He waits.

You almost lost your way with that tall blond girl with the cat. They asked me to step in. To keep you from loneliness and to help you to persevere. I was to teach you and inspire you.

Well, he says, you certainly did that. You all used me.

You could say that. It would also be true to say that they used us both.

But you knew, I didn't. And damn it all, I fell in love with you.

She looks down again into her glass and doesn't speak for a long time. She nods once, then shakes her head, then nods again and shakes her head again and finally she nods one last time and speaks.

I came to know what it means to fall in love, she says, and I will always treasure our time together. There will never be anything like it again in all my life.

And after that his anger has gone and the disappointment fades and all that remains is the sadness.

She again takes his glass and puts it and her own on the table next to the bottle and turns back to him and seeks his eyes and then reaches for him and they fall into the bedding and cling to one another in some desperate way and then begin tentatively to kiss and then kiss wildly and in the tangle of the bedding and his robe and her skimpy dress they escalate from desperation to passion still mixed with desperation and then she is on top of him and takes him into herself and they begin what they both know is to be the end. Sometime in the course of their coupling she sits upright still moving and removes the skimpy dress and helps him to remove his robe and they continue, prolonging this which they both know is to be the end, gripping each others' bodies where they can grip them, stroking every part of the other their hands can stroke, their eyes locked, he sees tears starting in hers and feels them starting in his own they are gripping and stroking not only each other but time itself, the world of the flesh and of the mind and spirit all at once, they are a single being in time and in the world as they thrust and rise and thrust and wait and rise and wait and thrust and wait until she begins to moan and he has to close his eyes trying to prolong this which they both know is the end and he cannot and she cannot either.

They remain joined, she astride him. She reaches down

and runs a finger through his tears and puts it to her mouth and tastes them. He reaches up and does the same and tastes hers. Their eyes are locked together and neither of them is willing or able to move.

There is one more thing you must know, she says.

What more is there to know than this? he asks.

Do you remember when you asked if I had a name I had earned, and I told you I had four?

Yes. One for flowers and one for tea and one for calligraphy. And one for everything else. That was Eisen. I remember.

You are Kansen-gobosan. That is your monk's name.

Yes.

She raises her arms slowly upward to her long and luxuriant black hair and puts her thumbs upward from her temples and pauses, still staring at him. Then she raises her hands and with them, hooked under her thumbs, she removes her long and luxuriant black hair and puts it aside on the tatami mat and folds her hands into the space where they are joined. Her head is completely shaven, just as his had been. She continues to hold his eyes and at last he understands.

Eisen-gobosan, he says.

Not gobo, she says. For a woman it is niso. But yes, I am a nun of the Senkyo convent near Kobê.

す

The morning bell wakes him. He has slept heavily. She is gone. Golden light streams in through the open window. He turns and sees that the sliding doors to the six-mat room are open too, and beyond, the sliding glass doors to the balcony are open as well. She wanted to be sure he would hear the bell, not be late getting to the airport.

He goes to the bathroom and showers long and hot, bending and stretching and hating that the water is stealing her scent from his body. Visions of her float past his closed eyes, with fragments of remembered dreams.

There is little time for this. The bell rang at six, he must be in a taxi by nine. He dries himself and racks the towel so it will dry and shaves carefully and puts on his sleeping robe. Puts on the kettle for tea, makes up the bedding, bags the used linens, finds a sheet of heavy, brownish paper lying on his half-packed kit. A poem in Chinese is brushed on it in her elegant hand. He takes out his dictionary, goes to the kitchen and while his tea steeps he hurriedly works out a translation on a sheet of scrap paper.

Friend Departing
Rihaku

Blue mountain still north of town,
White water flowing east of the castle.
This ground now used for departing,
By the orphan who will travel ten thousand leagues.
Thoughts of floating clouds, playing children.
As the sunset evokes human sentiment
My hand waves itself to him who leaves this place.
Sad, so sad, the horse's whinny.

There is no time for this. He darts his eyes around the kitchen, checks the fridge, turns it off, twists to dump its few contents into the trash but before he does he sees that she has left her red stiletto shoes and diaphanous red dress and long, black, luxuriant hair in the bin. He drops the leavings from the fridge on them. As he does he notices that she has also dumped yesterday's fresh flowers in the trash.

He dresses in his blue suit and a white shirt and blue tie and then stuffs a few more things into his pack, rolling the elegantly brushed poem carefully into the tube containing his sutras. The pack is his only luggage.

A cab waits in the turnaround under the shrine's arch. The ride to the Takamatsu airport takes less than an hour. He is given some grief over his expired visa at Immigration in Osaka, a note is stamped into his passport, but they let him go. He reads one of his paperbacks and walks the aisle often over the next several hours, trying not to doze, because when he dozes the first time he sees Kappa in a dark, black-and-white forest, threatening
him, insisting that West has betrayed him. West wakes from this with a start, stands quickly, grateful that he has an aisle seat and that the flight is not particularly crowded, and stumbles aft to the restroom. I have not betrayed you, I have done what I was asked to do. I have not betrayed you.

Later when he dozes again he meets the fox in the same dark forest. She snarls at him, hackles up and teeth bared. He wakes from this with a start too, but rather than standing and walking he sits confused. Why are you angry with me?

He reads a page of his paperback without any of the words registering. A meal is served, he eats tentatively, sushi with too much wasabi, weak green tea. When it has been cleared he returns to his book but drifts again. This time he looks into a cave where Senkyo-kai and Terayama Reikyo-kai sit face to face. The two mummified corpses turn and welcome him, beckon him to join them. He flees to the souvenir shop and seeks the counsel of the schoolboy, who wordlessly points to the door of the old woman at the other end of the shop. He goes to her door. It is not the old woman behind the door and it is not Mrs. Sakurada. It is Hanako. She says nothing, but hands him the antique key, which is no longer a key at all, but his brass sword guard with the Kappa worked into it.

These dreams and erotic images of Hanako pursue him through the San Francisco airport and to the Yamazaki dojo in the city where he collects his shipped things, his sword his inkstone the scrolls he has written his inks his brushes and much good

Japanese paper. Dreams and erotic images persist in the car across the desert and up to the borrowed cabin deep in the Rocky Mountain forest where he lives for a time as a hermit. There he meditates and writes the sutra every day and but for heavy snow one deeply bitter winter every day practices his karate and the drawing and sheathing of his sword.

He chops wood—for the stove.

He carries water—for the cistern.

And enjoys these tasks because they are easier than painting Kappa and the fox and the schoolboy and the little old woman at the souvenir shop and the heads of monks and the figures of mummies, in a strange style all his own, over and over, work as necessary to him as breath.

On moon-bright autumn nights when the coyotes yip and howl he lies on his pad and runs with them, yips and howls with them. On the mornings after he has run and yipped and howled with the coyotes he cannot paint Kappa or the fox or the schoolboy or the little old woman or the monks or the mummies but paints lewd pictures of Hanako instead and then burns them in his stove.

When those mornings are over he resumes painting the Kappa and the fox and the schoolboy and the rest until some years later when, running on the path in his split-toed boots into the forest above his cabin, he has just drawn his sword and cut an autumn mullen and sheathed and at last he understands both the paintings and the dreams and why Kappa and the fox have been angry with him. He knows that he *is* Kappa and he *is* the fox, and the schoolboy and the little old woman at the souvenir shop and Terayama and Hanako and Sendo and the birds and the great cedar and the clatter of wooden sandals and the sound of the bell and of the bamboo flute.

Knowing this at last frees him to follow the advice of the mummy, Senkyo-kai:

No need to believe anything. Just see.

This.

He knows he will spend the rest of an active and varied life learning to do exactly that.

Epilogue

West never returned to Takamatsu, never heard what happened to the people he knew there. The author can, however, tell the reader some of it.

The body of Reikyo-kai mummified perfectly, and three years later was taken from the cave, dressed in gold-shot red robes and mitre, and seated in the room facing Senkyo-kai. The two smile at each other, and don't have to say anything at all.

On the death of the soincho, Senkyo-gobosan succeeded to that position.

Hirano rose to high rank in Senkyo-ryu karate, and became its chief instructor.

Yamazaki-bucho continued in his pursuit of Suntory Old, to Miss Ota's despair. The offices above the computer shop in the Marugame-machi closed soon after West left. Mr. Okada retired, visited the offices of Time Magazine in New York, and took a ride on the Streetcar Named Desire in New Orleans.

Hanako Sakurada, as Eisen-niso, returned to the Senkyo convent near Kobê and resumed her seclusion as a nun. She was never again required to serve in the world.

Traditional holidays are still celebrated at the Hachiman shrine in Takamatsu. The trains of the JNR are still timed to avoid interfering with the bell above the cemetery when it rings the hours three times a day. And the bells throughout the city still ring in the New Year with their hundred and eight strokes.

A Note on the Chapter Headings

The symbols seen at the beginning of each chapter are those of the forty-eight Japanese phonetics called *Hiragana*, in which approximately seventy-percent of the Japanese language is written. In modern times, only forty-six are still used. Here, the old order of all forty-eight are used, forming the poem attributed to Kūkai, as described and roughly translated on page 137 of this edition. Note that the forty-eighth syllable ん (n), comes at the end of the story. This is because it is not a part of the poem as such, but is derived from the character, 无 (*nashi* or *mu*), which means "nothing," and is here used to mean "The End."

A Note on the Bell at Senkyō Temple

In Takamatsu the bells are rung on standard clock time— six at 6 AM, twelve at Noon, six again at 6 PM. At the mountain temple they are rung on ancient Chinese time, the hours actually two hours long, and named for the twelve animals of the Chinese zodiac. The fourth hour, for example, the Hour of the Hare, starts at 5 AM, lasts until 7AM, and is marked by four bells. The seventh hour, the Hour of the Horse, 11 AM to 1 PM, is marked by seven bells, etcetera.

A Few Other Notes

I have made an effort to use as few Japanese terms as possible. This has led to a certain awkwardness in places. The phrases "sit on the heels" or "sit formally" do not adequately describe *seiza*. "Split-toed cloth boots" is a fair description of *tobi-*

tabi, but fails to carry anything of the social implications of the footwear. "Wooden sandals" does not begin to describe *geta* properly. "Meditation" is a far too general a rendering of *zazen*. A *yukata* definitely is not merely a "sleeping robe." Several other examples of this sort arise in the book. I hope that, in translating these and other terms, I have made the story accessible to readers who are not familiar with Japan or Buddhism, and in doing so have not too seriously offended readers who are.

To my knowledge, no Senkyō sect exists. However, the existence of one by that name may be possible. Further, to my knowledge, no sect exists employing the same balance of practices or doctrines as does my invented Senkyō sect. Nevertheless, I consider it perfectly possible that one might.

The method of selecting Buddhist names within a given sect, as described on page 119 of this edition, is common in Japan.

The exchange of linked verses, in the format of an initial 5-7-5 syllable *haiku* (or at least haiku-like) verse, followed in response by a 7-7 syllable verse to complete a *waka* poem, is still practiced in Japan. All of those presented here are my own, scan as 5-7-5 and 7-7 in English, but probably cannot be translated into Japanese satisfactorily, and are unlikely to be real *haiku* or *waka* if they ever do happen to be translated. The translation of the Kukai poem and the translations of "Friend Departing" and Terayama-sensei's humorous extract from "Drinking Alone Under the Moon" by Rihaku (the Japanese pronunciation of Li Po, whose work is much loved in Japan) are my own (see "Notes on the Translations," pp. 239-243 below).

Although I had, much earlier, heard of self-mummification in the Chinese Taoist and Tibetan Buddhist traditions, I first heard of the Japanese Buddhist practice of it from a footnote in H. Byron Earhart's *A Religious Study of the Mount Haguro Sect of Shugendō*. That footnote referred to an article in *History of Religions*, "Self-Mummified Buddhas in Japan: An Aspect of the Shugen-dō

('Mountain Asceticism') Sect," by Ichiro Hori. It was from this article that I drew my description of the process Terayama follows in this book. Hanako's stories about the Mt. Koya monks being forced into the Japanese army were based on the reports in Brian Daizen Victoria's *Zen at War*.

Notes on the Translations

Translation is an art form requiring an understanding of two cultures as well as a literal knowledge of both languages. Every translation is an interpretation, and so will reflect the ethos of the culture and era in which it is made, and will also reflect the personal biases and beliefs of the translator, no matter how neutral he or she might try to be. A notable example of this is the translation of Fyodor Dostoevsky's *Besy* (1872). It was first translated into English in 1916 by an Englishwoman, Constance Garnett, under the title, *The Possessed*. This translation was found by numerous scholars to have distorted the book so severely that when it was re-translated in 1954 by David Magarshack, even the title had to be changed (to *The Devils*).

19th century Russian culture and language differed from those of England and Europe, but the differences are much less extreme than those between ancient China and the West, or medieval Japan and the West, so the translations of works from these cultures present even greater difficulties, especially in poetry and philosophy. I hope these notes will give the reader some idea of what is involved in that endeavor.

To begin, here are two translations of the *I-ro-ha* poem which the reader may compare with mine (on page 137):

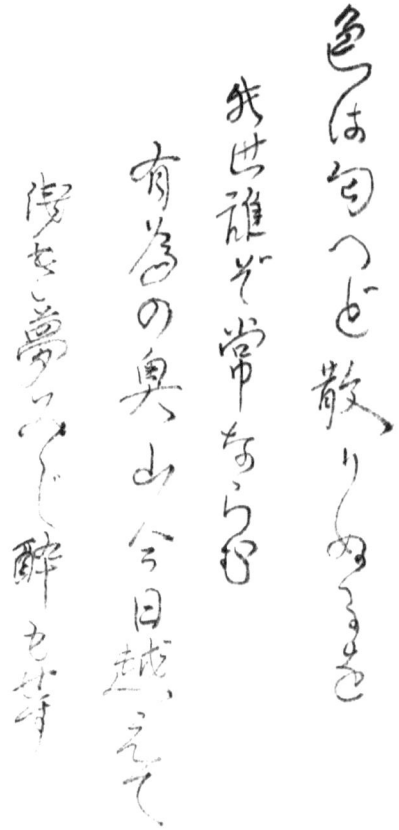

The I-Ro-Ha Poem written with *kanji* for Meanings

"Colors are fragrant, but they fade away. In this world of ours none lasts forever. Today cross the high mountain of life's illusions [i.e., rise above this physical world], and there will be no more shallow dreaming, no more drunkenness [i.e., there will be no more uneasiness, no more temptations]."

Andrew N. Nelson,
in his *Japanese-English Character Dictionary*

"Colour and perfume vanish away.
What can be lasting in this world?
Today disappears in the abyss of nothingness;
It is but the passing image of a dream, and
causes only a slight trouble."

Translator unknown; cited by Isabel Bird,
in her book, *Un-beaten Tracks in Japan*, 1880

Nelson's translation tries to render the poem literally, with the bracketed insertions attempting to interpret the related phrases in the Buddhist terms probably intended by the author. The one cited by Bird, however, seems to try to minimize the Buddhist influence. Bird did not speak fluent Japanese, so I assume the translation was made by her travel guide, or perhaps by the teacher at the school where she was visiting at the point in her book where the poem is quoted. Note the date: 1880. The events related in her book took place in the 1870s. This was early in the Meiji Period, when Japanese Buddhism was much deprecated and even somewhat suppressed by the government. (It is interesting to note this statement following the quoted poem):

". . . (the poem) indicates the singular Oriental distaste for life,
but is a dismal ditty for young children to learn. The Chinese classics,
formerly the basis of Japanese education, are now mainly taught as a
vehicle for conveying a knowledge of the Chinese character, in acquiring
even a moderate acquaintance with which the children undergo a great
deal of useless toil."

The contrast is, to me, intense. Nelson's understanding of the Japanese language and culture is profound. Bird's goes no further than *The Mikado*. My translation is loosely based on Nelson's, but geared to fit in with the situation in the story.

The Two Poems by LiPo (Rihaku)

There are several translations of "Under the Moon Alone Drinking" by Li Po. Both mine and the comical extract on page 96 are loosely derived from that of Ezra Pound, who, delightfully, translates it so that the poet accuses the moon of being drunk. This is not necessarily the poet's original intent, though it may have been. The poem taken as a whole, however, is not entirely comical. Here is my translation of the full text:

相永醉我找行暫影月對舉獨花
期結後舞歌樂伴徒既影杯酌間
邈無各影月須月隨不成邀無一
雲情分零徘乃將我解三明相壺
漢遊散亂徊春影身歡人月親酒

Alone Drinking Under the Moon
Among flowers, one jug of sakê
Alone drinking without friends
I offer cup to bright moon
Facing me, my shadow makes three of us
Moon already has no excuse for drinking
Shadow just follows my body
Moon brought shadow for company
Mirth should keep pace with Spring
I sing, crazy drunk moon spins
I dance, clumsy shadow tries dancing also
Let us enjoy this while drunk
Hungover, we'll all part
I can always rejoin my emotionless chums
I hope to meet again, in the distant realm of the clouds.

Here is a more accurate translation of *Friend Departing* than the one I offered (on page 230), wherein I excluded the military element as distracting from the story:

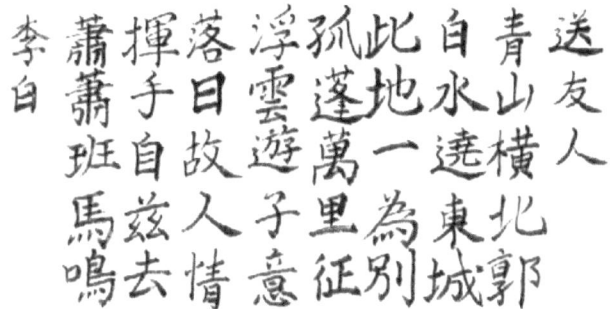

Blue mountain, unmoving north of town,
White water, flowing east of the castle.
This ground now used for departing
By the orphan who will travel ten thousand leagues to war.
Thoughts of floating clouds, playing children,
As the sunset evokes human sentiment.
My hand waves itself to him who leaves this place.
Bleak, bleak, the whinny of the troop's horses.

Note "unmoving" here, rather than the "still" on page 230. I did this because of the questionable nature of Time in the story, "still" having a temporal element to it. The character involved literally means "beside," or "to the side." There may have been political and philosophical implications to the poem when written, but I have chosen to ignore them in these translations, so as to emphasize instead the sadness of parting. "To war" might also be rendered as "on patrol," an historical question. The "bleak" here in the last line is more literal than the "sad" on page 230. The more literal translation of the character I've offered as "whinny" is "cry out" or "call out," and not specific to horses.

Three Lines from the Heart Sutra (*Shingyō*)

Of all of the texts translated in the book, the excerpts from the *Shingyō* (The Heart Sutra) are the most problematic. The sutra has been translated many times in various periods and by translators from diverse religious, philosophical, and scholarly backgrounds. There are many lengthy commentaries, histories, and explanations of it in a great variety of contexts. In *In this Living Body* I quoted three phrases from the *Shingyō*, each intended to enhance or illustrate an element of the story, rather than to elucidate the sutra itself. My monograph, *Shingyō: Reflections on Translating the Heart Sutra* (Silverback Sages, Publishers, 2013) contains the entire text in Sino-Japanese, with romanized Sino-Japanese pronunciations approximate literal meanings in English, notes and comments.

摩訶般若波羅蜜多心経

ma -		to polish
	}Note 1	
ka		to proclaim
han- Note 2.		carry
-nya		young
ha -		wave
-ra-		silk gauze
-mi-		honey; nectar
-ta		many
shin Note 3.		
gyō		classic or sacred text

1. As part of the title, these two characters are used simply to render the Sanskrit sounds, *maha*. Here, as in all such cases following, it is of much interest to note the meanings of the characters chosen to represent the sounds.

2. The same is true of the next five characters in the title. These render the Sanskrit *"Prajna Paramita"*. This is usually translated as "Highest Wisdom", but the way it is frequently used in this text suggests that it here it may mean "meditation".

3. *shin*:

  Does "Heart" properly translate *"hridaya"* as it was meant or understood in Sanskrit? Does "Heart" properly translate the Chinese character *"shin"*? For that matter, did *"shin"* properly translate the word from Sanskrit to Chinese in the first place? I have often encountered this character translated into English as "heart/mind" in the Japanese tradition, and, recently, found "heart/mind" as the translation of the related Thai term. Most commentators translate the Chinese *"shin"* as "mind" rather than "heart". All this seems to me to be evidence that the distinction we draw between heart and mind is not the same one drawn in these Buddhist and pre-Buddhist cultures, if they in fact draw any distinction between the two concepts at all. This character is used twice more in the document. It occurs in the phrase translated into English as, "no obstructions, therefore, mind having no fear", and at the very end, *"Hannya Shingyō"* (which can be taken as a reprise of the title). In any case, it is usually translated as "mind" in the phrase in the main text, and as "heart" in the title and the reprise. This seems to indicate that, while the Chinese considered the character to have one meaning in both contexts, the translators into English have needed two words for it.

Another phrase from the *Shingyō* appears on 89ff, and again in both English and Sino-Japanese on page 109. Only the third group of four characters (*shiki soku ze kū*) is actually quoted:

色	*shiki*	color; sensuality
不	*fu*	not
異	*i*	different
空	*kū*	sky; space; emptiness
空	*kū*	sky; space; emptiness
不	*fu*	not
異	*i*	different
色	*shiki*	color; sensuality
色	*shiki*	color; sensuality
即	*soku*	exact(ly)
是	*ze*	this; thus
空	*kū*	sky; space; emptiness
空	*kū*	sky; space; emptiness
即	*soku*	exact(ly)
是	*ze*	this; thus
色	*shiki*	color; sensuality

This is probably the most frequently quoted phrase from the text, and probably the most difficult. To start with, all the translators I've found (except one which gives us "body") give "form" for *shiki*. While *shiki* (using this character) has indeed several meanings, in all my dictionaries they fall in one way or another under the categories I've offered here. There are two or three characters which mean "form" quite clearly, in many or all contexts (e.g. 形 , 型). Further, later, as will be noted, the character *shiki* is used in other contexts, where the translation is not form, but "color" or, in one version, "objects of sight." I used "form" in the book, just because it is the most common translation, but I think that in this context, the entire world of the senses is intended.

On the other hand, *kū* is almost always given in English as "emptiness." Mu,* in his interpretive commentary, expands on "emptiness" at great length, making it clear that he considers it vital and essential to an understanding of the text as a whole.

* Mu Soeng Sunim: *Heart Sutra: Ancient Buddhist Wisdom in the Light of Quantum Reality.*

Primary Point Press, 1991.

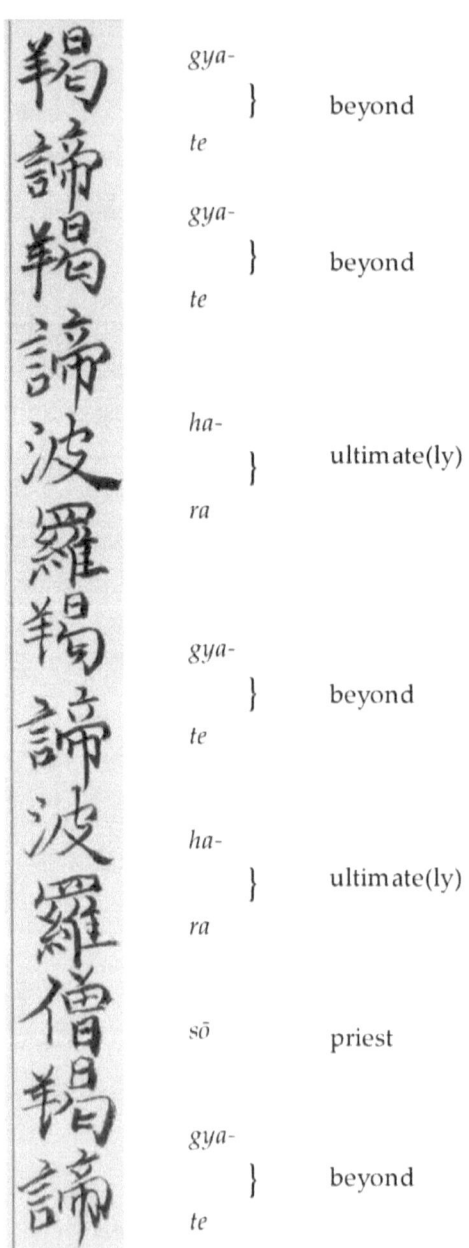

gya-
} beyond
te

gya-
} beyond
te

ha-
} ultimate(ly)
ra

gya-
} beyond
te

ha-
} ultimate(ly)
ra

sō   priest

gya-
} beyond
te

This is the third and last direct quotation from the *Shingyō*, which I translated in the book as "Beyond, beyond, even beyond Beyond, goeth the priest." This is based on my understanding of a translation by Allen Ginsberg, and is perhaps somewhat more poetic than literal, but seems to carry the emotional element appropriate to the story at that point.

In the few lines of the sutra preceding the phrase, it is referred to as a *shu*, which is a translation of the Sanskrit *dharani* (some versions), or *mantra*. That is to say, all of the translations have left the word un-translated. The dictionaries give us "Spell, Curse, or Incantation." In this context, I think we can assume it to refer to a sound, word, or phrase intoned to help open the mind to meditation. Other examples of *shu* are *Om Mani Padme Hūm* from Tibet, and *Namu Amida Butsu* from the Jōdō Buddhist sect in Japan. Of such, the single syllables *Om, Aom,* and *Mu* are probably the most common.

Two more Phrases from the *Shingyō*

While not quoted in the book, the two phrases from the *Shingyō* below were, to a large degree, the inspiration for Senkyō-kai's statement on page 195 and repeated on the last page. "No need to believe anything" is clearly not a faithful translation of the phrase, but the reader may see the relevance after reading the Notes on "*hō* and "*sō*":

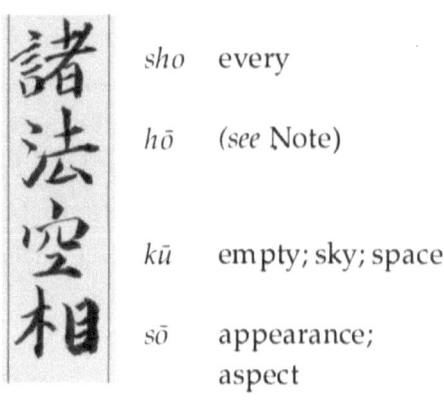

sho	every	
hō	(*see* Note)	
kū	empty; sky; space	
sō	appearance; aspect	

hō: In other than Buddhist contexts, this is usually translated as "Rules, methods, laws, etc." In the Buddhist context, it is a rendering of "Dharma". A solid definition of "Dharma" appears to be complicated. The Dalai Lama gives "phenomena". Dr. C.W. Swain suggests that "teachings" might be accurate. Another alternative might be "received wisdom." W.T. Chan gives us "that which is held to." Perhaps, then, in this context, it may mean "belief." (Dr. Swain insists that it does not mean "belief." I'm not certain if our definitions of the word "belief" agree. I define belief as a proposition, statement, or assumption, which cannot be verified or falsified, proven or disproven, yet is held as true. Of the current English translations, most leave the word "Dharma" un-translated, and one skips the phrase entirely.)

This character *sō* (相) also has several meanings, which clearly change as contexts change. However, it often implies "similar to," "corresponding to" or "reciprocal." It is composed of two elements, "wood" or "tree" on the left, "eye" on the right. The "wood"element often implies "real," "actual," "material" (as opposed to "imaginary"). When the *shin* element is added to 相, as in *ju sō* (想) *gyo shiki* and, later, in *musō* (夢想), the meaning becomes "imagined," "mental," or some other concept having to do with mind.

Here is the phrase from the *Shingyō* that inspired Senkyō-kai's "Just see", and West's eventual understanding of it to mean "Just see *this*." It has always struck me that this phrase is an exhortation to perceive with a completely open mind and heart.

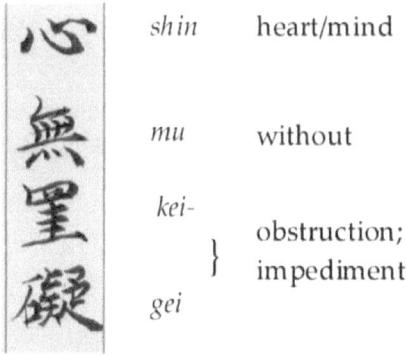

shin	heart/mind	
mu	without	
kei-	}	obstruction; impediment
gei		

Acknowledgements

I am deeply grateful to Jim Horne Minter, whose long friendship and editing skills saw me through this book, and, in fact, through all the books before. Thanks also to William (Bill) Baynes, whose reading led to a revival of spirits, as well as to several important changes and corrections. Thanks too to my cousin, Dr. Mary Sullivan, whose psychological insight spared me a couple of severe errors, and to Takeshi Ikeuchi-*sensei*, of Takamatsu University, who helped me to correct certain cultural mistakes. Several other readers were kind enough to read the book's many drafts, and to offer valuable comments and corrections. Thanks to Nancy Mack and Jim Minter, III. as well, whose computer skills turned a manuscript into an actual printed book.

I am most grateful to Dr. Charles W. Swain, and to the library of the Florida State University for access to Dr. Earhart's book, and to many others, especially the R. F. C. Hull translations of C. G. Jung's *Alchemical Studies, Psychology and Alchemy,* and *Psychology and Religion,* which have significantly influenced this book and, indeed, the whole of my adult life.

I have wanted to write a book without quotation marks ever since reading my first Cormac McCarthy novel. He is not the only modern American writer to leave them out: Peter Matthiessen's masterpiece, *Far Tortuga,* had none, nor did Kent Haruf's *Plainsong, Eventide,* and *Benediction,* for example. Reading these books, I thought long and hard about why the lack of quote marks so enhanced them. I decided that it was because it sustained the stream of consciousness, giving the entirely interior narrative mode a poetic and dream-like feeling. This was exactly the effect I wanted for *In this Living Body.* I am immensely grateful to Mr. McCarthy, and others using the technique, for freeing American fiction from the essentially journalistic convention of quotation marks.

And, as ever and as always, I am grateful for my dearest Herta. Without her love, and my love for her, *In this Living Body* would never have come to life.

M. J. Sullivan has been a concert guitarist, a teacher, a sailing captain and an artist. He has a BA in Humanities and an MA in Asian Studies. *WAZA*, his first novel about Japanese Buddhism and the martial arts, received the CoVisions Recognition Award for Literature.

He earned the name Seihō and his teacher's license in calligraphy from Nippon Shuji Kyōiku Zaidan, and wrote the English language versions of their textbooks. He was made an Honorary Citizen of Takamatsu and one year was the *nidan* level swordsmanship champion of Kagawa Prefecture.

Deeply involved with Zen and Japanese culture, he paints and writes at Tōshoin (洞　書　院, Cave Writing Hall), his studio in the Colorado Rocky Mountains.

www.ingramcontent.com/pod-product-compliance
Lightning Source LLC
Chambersburg PA
CBHW032025240626
47154CB00003B/793